DRAGON DAD'S NANNY

DRAGON DAD'S LOVE CHRONICLES

AMELIA WILSON

Earning trust and love is easy, keeping it is harder.

Sam has no doubt in his mind that he will whatever it takes to keep his daughters safe. If that means giving custody to his ex-wife, then he will do it. However, the girls are not yet fully grown, and no one knows whether they are shifters. That puts them in danger. What's more, the girls are attached to their babysitter, and it might just break everyone's heart if Sam's ex wins this battle.

AnnaLee has found her life is filled with satisfaction when she is watching Emma and Jose, Sam's twin girls. They are spunky and are a part of AnnaLee's life that she never thought she would get to have. Now one doctor's note haunts her, and the custody papers she finds on the kitchen counter are haunting her even more.

The history Sam has with his ex-wife is dangerous and filled with secrets.

The hope and love that swell like tidal wives between AnnaLee and Sam are addictive and nearly overpower any reservations they might have. Both of them are willing to do whatever it takes to keep the family they are becoming together.

More than one heart: one family is on the line, and they are willing to risk it all.

SAM

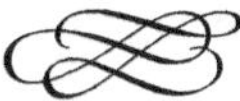

The girls were still running around in their nightgowns, screaming about the tickle monster that Sam was feeling less than at the moment. It was their morning wake-up routine. Sam didn't believe in giving his girls alarms, other than his tickling fingers that prodded and pulled them out of bed, their eyes as wide as saucers, begging for juice and whatever scrumptious breakfast Sam had made.

He never had to deal with a groggy child. Unfortunately they often had to deal with a groggy dad. The coffee machine was slow, and the drip had just started. The faint smell of the Caribbean coffee and the sound of the plop on the bottom of the pot were almost enough to calm his nerves and wake him up completely.

Sam was very rarely nervous. However, he *was* nervous when he met Cain, who had asked him to join the Dragon PI team, *and* when the girls were born, *and* the first day he had left them with AnnaLee, *and* today. God above, he hadn't even had his coffee yet, and he was already jittery and bouncing on his toes.

Maybe he needed to be the tickle monster for a few minutes more, to work off the building adrenaline.

"Daddy!" Jose screamed her way between his legs and the counter.

He could not imagine that the cupboard handle digging into her back was comfortable, but she remained there and stared up at him.

"What is it, baby girl?" he asked. Surprisingly, his girls relaxed him more than coffee ever could. They were consistent; although, depending on how things went today, that could change.

"I don't want cereal," she said.

"Baby girl, I don't have time to make pancakes or eggs today," Sam said. He looked behind himself and watched Emma haul herself into one of the dining room chairs, where she sat pounding her fists on the wood. "Emma, don't hit the table!"

He swung Jose up into his arms, and sat her down next to Emma. "Alright, girls, number one – which I tell you daily – don't hit the table. Number two, pick a cereal."

There wasn't a chance he was even going to open the table to a breakfast debate, and he wasn't going to try to give them a healthy cereal. They were balls of energy this morning and his best chance was to give them more sugar and let AnnaLee take care of them.

"Lucky Charms!" Emma yelled.

"Cinnamon Toast Crunch with a real cinnamon toast!" Jose said, banging a fist on the table for emphasis.

Did he slam his hands on tables? Were they copying him, because he couldn't imagine where else they'd picked it up from?

Sam looked at Jose's hand pointedly and back up at her. She smiled and spread her fingers on the table. Sam quickly grabbed her hand and pretended to gobble it up, bringing forth a fresh burst of laughter from the girls.

Even if he was stressed, he wouldn't show it around them. There was no need for them to feel as worried as he was, or to be concerned about his unusual attitude.

When the coffee was percolated and the sound of the cereal slushing into the glass dinosaur bowls (handpicked by the girls) quietened, Sam dared a glance at the clock. It was a quarter past ten. If he was going to make it to the courthouse on time, he needed to leave now. Why wasn't AnnaLee here?

She was never late, so where the hell was she? Did her alarm not go off? Did she forget?

He planted the cereal bowls in front of his girls, and rushed to fill his travel mug. He skipped over the sugar and cream, deciding he didn't have the time. He slipped his cell from his pocket and was half way through dialing Samia's number when the front door opened.

AnnaLee breezed in with rosy cheeks and the smell of magnolias and petrichor. He could tell by the light sheen on her forehead and the hair sticking to her cheeks that it was muggy outside.

She stretched a smile across her face and said, "Good Morning! Sorry I'm late."

Before she could reach the girls and give them both kisses on the cheeks, Sam was scowling and marching past her. "Next time, a heads up would be nice."

"I'm sorry, I—"

"You're not the only one with something to do in the morning AnnaLee!"

"Yes, but—"

"It's inconsiderate of you not to call," he said his voice significantly lower as he remembered the girls in the other room.

"I'm sorry. I'll remember to call next time."

"See that you do, because I don't have a problem finding another nanny."

AnnaLee crossed her arms at this bold statement. She said, "Oh? You can quickly find another nanny with as much experience as I have and whom your daughters accept so well?"

He knew what she said was right. She was one of a kind. A blessing he could never imagine finding anywhere else.

Unfortunately, at that moment, he was stressed out and seeing red. Speaking intelligently was impossible. "Yes," he said.

She picked up her keys where she'd dropped them on the counter and shoved past him toward the door. "Have fun missing whatever you're late for then, and enjoy nanny searching."

He sucked in a breath. "AnnaLee, don't set a foot out that door unless you are willing to say goodbye forever."

He was surprised when she froze. She turned around and said, "Look, I apologized, but I don't need to be treated this way."

Sam stomped past her and yelled over his shoulder, "Just call next time, ok?" He was already out and slamming the door.

He winced as the door closed behind him. The girls had never heard him close a door so harshly, nor had they ever heard him talk so curtly to AnnaLee. Later he would explain and apologize for his actions.

He gunned out of the driveway and raced through the neighborhood eager to make up the lost time.

Today, Sam and his ex-wife were sitting down and discussing having a child custody evaluation. As much as Sam loved his daughters, it was out of his love for them that he was beginning to question whether he was the correct parent for them to live with.

The first custody battle had been rough. The girls were barely out of the hospital, and the only way he won was because the court was convinced their mom wouldn't be home often enough to raise them properly. Now Sam was the one traveling almost every other weekend, and asking AnnaLee to stay nights with the girls while he was away. He didn't think that was fair, and if the girls could have a chance to be with their mother, he wanted to give it to them.

The dinosaur bowls were enough evidence that the girls had too much masculine influence in their lives. While the girls were often around Nora, Samia, Harper, and AnnaLee none of them were the girls' mother, and that's what they needed. Jose and Emma needed the stable influence of a mother; a mother who could fix them pancakes everyday or force the healthy-cereal-only rule, because some days Sam had a hard time even waking them up and getting them out of bed.

Like today. Today was a hard day.

He parked the car and bounded up the courthouse steps. He found his way down the old, familiar halls to Conference Room C. He stood outside the door for a few heartbeats, before walking in.

It was five years since he'd seen his ex-wife. He didn't know what he expected when he walked in, but he was pleasantly relieved by the smile she gave him, wan as it was.

"Hi Sam," Jordan said, and she stood and held a hand out to him as if they were old business partners. He supposed they were, if the job was making a family and quickly abandoning it upon completion.

"Jordan," he said a little more tersely than he intended. His gut twisted at the sight of her. He kept one hand around his coffee cup and the other in his pocket.

The evaluator and their attorneys stood watching the interaction. After a moment of silence, the evaluator held a hand out to a chair on the opposite side of the table to Jordan.

"Mr. Lorin, please have a seat."

Sam nodded his head in acknowledgment and sat down. He was thankful that for once his suit didn't sport a stain of milk, coffee, or marker anywhere on the jacket or the pants. He hadn't bothered looking for a tie, but thought he still looked professional enough.

The evaluator introduced himself as Michael Thurshin. He was a tall man, built like an electric post, with wire frame glasses pushed under his eyebrows. His hair was speckled gray, and Sam wondered how many cases he handled a day. Thurshin couldn't be more than thirty-six, and yet he carried himself as if he was in his sixties.

Thurshin pressed on the bridge of his glasses, as if they could go up any higher. "I know why we're here, but I would like both of you to state why you're here to make sure we are all on the same page. Sam?"

This was a statement Sam had run through his head a hundred times. It was his justification for giving up the lights of his life so they could keep shining.

"My job keeps me busy and often takes me out of the country, sometimes for several weeks. It's a dangerous job, and I cannot guarantee that I will come back alive, therefore I believe I'm providing an unstable family unit and environment for Emma and Jose to grow up in." Some of the words seemed to get stuck in his throat, like swallowing a spoonful of peanut butter, and they dripped slowly off his tongue like syrup.

They were bitter flavors to him.

"So you don't want the children?" Thurshin asked.

Sam held his breath for just a moment, to school his features and calm his heart, betrayed by only himself. "Of course, I want the girls, but I don't think I'm a suitable dad for them at this time."

"And you, Jordan, do you want the kids?"

A moment too long passed before Jordan spoke. A moment in which Sam remembered when the twins were born, crying and shaking their fists in the air. Jordan wouldn't even look at them or hold them.

The anger Sam had felt then began to stir again, and he struggled to keep it down. Of all of his friends, Sam was the relaxed one. He was good at not getting into fights, but it didn't mean he didn't want to.

As with any dragon, he had a furnace within him, constantly begging to be stoked. Sam had just learned to deny its most basic pleasures.

"Yes," Jordan said. The word came out tumbling out on a shuddered breath.

After all these years, now she wanted the girls. Sam ground his teeth together. He really had no right to be mad, considering he was offering the girls to her.

Sam was the one who had called for the evaluation. He only had himself to blame.

"I'm here because I regret my lack of involvement as a mother. Over the past five years I've worked to establish a business in the city and to create a safe home in the hope that I can have the twins over."

"And are you ready to have them full time?" Thurshin was not wasting a second of this meeting.

There was another hesitated second before Jordan said yes.

"Excellent," Thurshin began, "then let's start talking about what these evaluations will look like, and how they will take place."

ANNALEE

The door slamming behind her felt like a grip on her spine that pulled her straight and held her breath in the latch. She had done nothing to upset Sam, but it was still hard not to take it personally.

AnnaLee braced a hand on the counter and pressed her other hand to her stomach. As much as it probably messed up Sam's morning for her to be late, her morning was ruined long before she even woke up. Today was destined to be bad.

"Did Daddy leave?" Emma peeked into the kitchen looking for the source of the slamming door.

These girls had never known an argument outside of their own. Sure, there had been times in the past when AnnaLee and Sam didn't agree on something, but they never let their voices rise and shake the house. The worst that had ever happened to the girls was tripping on the sidewalk and scrapping their knees.

"Yes, he did, pumpkin." AnnaLee swept Emma up into her arms.

Emma's bottom lip trembled as she said, "He didn't say goodbye."

Oh Sam, whatever had him so wound up had him forgetting the most important daily ritual: kissing the girls a goodbye on the cheek.

"He was in a hurry, but he asked me to kiss you both for him." She pressed her lips to Emma's cheek as the girl squealed and slid from AnnaLee's hands. Catching Jose before she slipped from the table, she planted a kiss on Jose's cheek.

"What did you both have for breakfast?"

"Cereal!" they yelled.

AnnaLee flinched at the volume of their voices and the breakfast choice. Sam made it his duty to cook for the girls as often as he could. If he gave them cereal then he was in a rush like none AnnaLee had ever seen before.

Guilt began to swim in her stomach.

No, she told herself. She didn't need to feel guilty. Circumstances beyond her control had kept her from arriving on time.

The girls were about to dart upstairs and find toys to litter the floors, but AnnaLee called, "Wait, take your dishes to the sink!"

The girls bowed their heads, caught trying to escape from their chores. Dutifully they returned and obeyed.

AnnaLee followed them into the kitchen. Once the bowls were in the sink, she handed each girl a banana. They needed at least one healthy thing for breakfast.

"Go make your beds and wash up for the day. Put on overalls, so we can go outside." She gave them a wink, a mischievous act to make them wonder at what fun she had planned for the day.

What the girls would interpret as treasure hunting would be AnnaLee putting them to work weeding in the garden. Sam never bothered with the garden, but it was one of the first things AnnaLee noticed when she became the nanny for the girls. Over the past year or so, she had put some attention into it, and now it was blooming. She loved the look of it, but it needed to be tamed, so today was a day for weeding.

Afterwards she would have the girls put on their bathing suits, and while she watered the plants she would also spray the girls. Emma and Jose had so much energy, AnnaLee had to be creative in finding ways to help them spend it. Too many nights the girls were still running wild well past their bedtime.

Once the banana peels were in the trash and the girls were in their rooms, AnnaLee sat herself on the bar stool at the island in the kitchen and dropped her head into her hands.

Two weeks ago, she'd a doctor's appointment. She had always had the worst period cramps her whole life, and lately they had become unbearable. She should have gotten them checked out when she was younger, but it had only occurred to her two weeks ago.

Today, she'd gotten the test results back. In short, she couldn't have kids. It was the most devastating news she'd ever had. A dream she had had since she was Emma and Jose's age was destroyed in a matter of seconds.

Three large fibroids were attached to her uterus. They'd probably been there for years, steadily growing, until her menstrual pains were so severe this last time that she finally went to the doctor.

She'd smiled at her doctor, pressed her lips thin, and nodded her thanks for taking his time to tell her. But when she got to the car, she sobbed, unable to contain the emotions that flooded her endlessly. They were dull now, but they still roared in her ear.

It was something she had suspected for a while. About a year ago, AnnaLee and her boyfriend at the time were trying to conceive, but nothing ever came from their attempts except a satisfying sex life. Although it couldn't have been that good for him, because he left her.

An image of a glass fruit bowl sliding off a counter and shattering, bruising all the fruit in its crash landing crossed her mind. She couldn't tell if she was the bowl, the bruised fruit, or the careless elbow that knocked the bowl down. Whichever she was, she imagined that as the pain she felt.

She was cracked beyond repair. She was a bruised apple no one wanted to eat. She was guilty, a failure of a woman.

She pressed the palms of her hands to her eyes, willing the tears to stay locked up. She could hear rushing feet coming down the stairs.

"Before we go outside, I *will* check your bedrooms!"

The feet paused and hurried back upstairs.

AnnaLee combed her fingers back through her hair and released the shuddering breaths clanging and clamoring from her lungs up her throat. She had cried in the car, so if she needed to cry again, it could wait until later.

Stepping out of the kitchen, she stomped her way slowly up the stairs. She heard the girls scream, scrambling to finish decorating their beds. When AnnaLee walked into Emma's room first, she found both girls on the floor, with barrettes littered between them.

The mass of barrettes were glittery butterflies and flowers, which they had clipped in each others clumsily braided hair. They looked like wild garden children, and AnnaLee supposed she had no one but herself to blame for that. She had taught them how to braid their hair well enough, so she didn't have to do it, and the girls were rarely allowed to play inside when the weather was nice.

AnnaLee glanced up from them and saw the neatly made bed. "Good job, Emma Fairy Child," AnnaLee said. She pointed a finger at Jose, "Time for your room."

Jose's bed was just as well made. "Jose Fairy Child, you also did well. Clean up the clips girls, and let's go outside; we have treasure to find!"

The sound of treasure was enough to get the girls rushing to scoop the hair clips into a basket. A beat ahead of AnnaLee, the girls raced down the stairs and out the back door, stopping at AnnaLee's garden basket to grab their little trowels.

AnnaLee should have chastised them for running down the stairs. Sam was paranoid they would fall and hurt themselves, but already, AnnaLee was too exhausted to get after them. Let them run, she thought.

The sun was high and had them all sweating through their clothes in minutes. AnnaLee was constantly sitting back on her heels from weeding, to wipe the dripping sweat from her forehead, trying to keep it from stinging her eyes. The girls were undeterred, finding small little polished rocks AnnaLee would often scatter around the flowers during their naps.

The laughter ringing from the girls was like music to AnnaLee's ears as she worked. Time sped up, and before they knew it, it was time for lunch.

"Emma! Jose!" AnnaLee called over her shoulder.

"Coming!" They called from the other end of the garden.

AnnaLee pulled her gardening gloves off her hand, finger by finger, and slapped them against her leg to shake the dirt off them before tucking them into her back pocket. Turning toward the house, the girls met her halfway. "Time for some fairy lunches," AnnaLee said.

The girls clapped their hands, jumping for joy.

"Do you want a caterpillar or ants on a log?"

The girls gave each other one look before speaking together as loud as they could, "Caterpillar!"

AnnaLee laughed, allowing the joy of the girls to seep into her bones. The garden work was good for distracting her from the morning's disappointment, but she would need to rely on the girl's abounding energy and light to get her through the rest of the day.

Inside, the girls rushed to wash their hands then sat down in the dining room. AnnaLee gave them cardstock paper, glue sticks, and fairy coloring pages for them to decorate with the crayons and rhinestones she scattered about the table. Once they were occupied, she moved to the kitchen to make their lunch.

Peanut butter and jelly sandwiches were cut into the shape of a house. Strawberry slices made up the shingled roof, and a chocolate square was placed as the door. A carrot became the chimney, and almonds were scattered as a pathway.

Finally came the caterpillar. AnnaLee cut a banana in half along the side and spread peanut butter along the rounded edge. For the finishing touch, she sprinkled dark chocolate chips over the peanut butter.

Emma and Jose pushed their mess to the middle of the table when AnnaLee came out to give them their lunches. "What do you want to drink girls?"

"Apple juice," Emma said.

"Milk," Jose said.

"Apple juice and milk, coming right up." AnnaLee retrieved the drinks and her own lunch from the counter. She had made herself a similar fairy lunch.

Throughout lunch, the girls continued to work on their craft. AnnaLee helped by cutting shapes from the card stock and complimenting their individual designs. By the time lunch was finished, the girls were ready to settle down for a short time.

Moving to the living room, AnnaLee downloaded several episodes of the Bakyardigans. The first episode was nearly over by the time the girls fell asleep. Their heads had both claimed AnnaLee's legs.

She gently ran her fingers through their hair, and sat through the rest of the episode. She wondered if she should risk moving the girls. Wake one of them up now and they would be up the rest of the day.

These naps were still crucial to their development. They were getting shorter and shorter, but they were still important for the girls' depleted energy. And it made dinnertime so much nicer.

AnnaLee could count a handful of times when dinner had turned into a food fight between the twins. They're emotions were at such extremes, it was astonishing. When they were happy, they were exuberant; when they were down, it was either a fiery rage or tears that fell in rivalry with Niagara Falls.

It took AnnaLee a long time to learn to read the girls' cues and until they developed a steady routine that helped them balance any emotions, they were feeling. AnnaLee almost wanted to laugh when she saw Sam's face the first day he worked from home and had asked her to come in. His jaw had nearly dropped to the floor when he watched the girls singing their own cleaning song, while washing their hands and rinsing their snack cups.

"I didn't even know it was possible to get children to clean," Sam had said.

AnnaLee had laughed then. She said it was important to delegate small tasks to them while they were young. It gave them a sense of independence, helped the parents, but also showed that chores or work could be fun.

Even though the memory was a good one, AnnaLee didn't feel any laughter now. Which was good considering the slumbering beasts on her lap, but she wondered if she would ever feel like laughing again.

The second episode started, and AnnaLee was careful to shift the girls off her so she could get up. Retreating to the kitchen, she grabbed a glass of water and gulped it down. It should have felt refreshing, but it only seemed to give more fuel to the fresh tears building behind her lashes.

Dead dreams rose in her mind again. It was hard to believe that it was only this morning that they had been slaughtered by a diagnosis. She imagined little faces beginning to disintegrate, and researched baby names were erased.

She shoved those to the back of her mind. Not today. She wasn't ready to do that today.

To forget.

To start over and find a new dream.

AnnaLee refilled her glass of water, drinking it more slowly this time. After washing it and placing it on the drying rack, she peeked in on the girls, and quietly tiptoed to the little office room, close to the back of the house.

Slipping inside, she saw the familiar tall bookshelves that lined three of the four walls in the room. The floor was a beautiful hardwood with a soft shag rug placed in the center. A single blue recliner was stationed on top of the rug with a small table placed next to it.

She couldn't pinpoint when or what drove her to find this room and take solace in it, but she did. She imagined Sam did too, which is why he had it designed this way. It was quiet, and despite being closed off, it didn't feel crowded.

She wondered what drove Sam to this room.

His job probably, not that he ever told her anything.

Sam had caught her in the room once before, returning a book she had borrowed. She stammered to explain herself, but he held up his hand and told her to take her time while he went to check on the girls. When she left, she could see in his eyes that he understood the need for solitude and space, and he had never asked her anything beyond to be careful with the books and to keep the floor clean of any crumbs.

He never told her anything, and she never told him anything. It didn't matter when they fit in each others lives so easily. The girls were like her own daughters.

Daughters she would never have, now.

AnnaLee raked a hand through her hair. She needed to distract herself.

She quickly slipped a book off the shelves and returned to the living room, but by the time she got back, Emma was already waking up.

The girls spent the next forty minutes bleary eyed and watching TV, until they asked for a snack. Once they had eaten and changed out of their overalls into shorts and t-shirts, they made a quick trip grocery shopping, because there was no way AnnaLee was going to leave their cupboards as bare as they were, or the fruit bowl as empty as it was. Sam was a great dad, but he forgot to go shopping until the last minute.

AnnaLee made it her personal goal to make sure everything was stocked for him and the girls. It wasn't without its perks, since AnnaLee did eat there half the time.

When they returned from shopping, it was a slow afternoon of reading and coloring, finishing final touches on the fairy houses to add them to the fridge, and before they knew it, it was dinnertime. Grabbing a blanket and paper plates, they ate in the yard, enjoying the dip of the sun and the peek-a-boo stars behind the drifting clouds.

As soon as the yard was cleaned, the girls tramped dutifully upstairs to brush their teeth and faces before collapsing into their beds. AnnaLee pulled the covers to their chins and kissed them goodnight on the forehead, before she collapsed on the couch.

She shifted in her seat, already her stamped out thoughts coming back. She had never been good at handling the bombardment of thoughts that pestered her in moments like these. They were persistent and drove her insane.

Not tonight.

She burst from the couch and moved to the reading room. Taking a knitted blanket with her, she curled up into the chair and let her mind drift with the story she had chosen from the shelves.

15

SAM

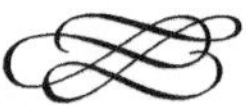

anging his head on the steering wheel would not help anything, but with each thud against the warm leather, Sam hoped it would. He hoped it would push the memories to the back of his mind. He hoped it would drown out the sound of his ex-wife laughing.

That laugh used to be the only thing that held him together. It used to be gentle. Now it mocked him, and pulled each delicately sewn thread in his heart until it was splitting in two again.

He squeezed his eyes tight and held his breath.

"Sam, what are you doing?" Jordan had laughed.

The memory was from when they had taken a vacation up in the mountains. It was late spring, and the mountainside was covered in wildflowers. It was a steadily dipping slope, and Jordan had practically run down, almost stumbling and falling the rest of the way.

When they had stopped, she knelt in the tall growing stalks of flowers and began to snap their stems to create a bouquet. Sam held his breath and refused to blink, convinced that was the only way he could commit the image of her to memory.

It had worked too well, if now he was holding his breath while he kept his eyes closed to erase it. That was one of the few good memories of their relationship. Most of the time they were fighting. Fighting to make things work, because he was a dragon shifter and she was a shifter hunter.

When Sam had found out what Jordan had dedicated her life to, it was hard for him to believe. Likewise, it was hard for Jordan to stomach his being a dragon. They were so convinced they could make it work though. Their marriage was rocky, but it officially fell apart when Jordan became pregnant.

Too many nights and arguments revolved around what would happen if the kids were shifters. Jordan didn't want to get rid of them in case the babies were normal, but if they weren't she would hate herself forever for being the one to bring them into the world.

Sam sat back in his car, and watched Jordan exit the courthouse. She looked at him from where she stood before moving to her car.

This process was going to be long and it would not be easy. Sam had no doubt in his mind that Jordan was making plans to hunt him, as soon as she had the girls. If Sam lost the girls, even though he was the one who had recommended the re-evaluation, he didn't think he would stop Jordan.

He shook his head. These were not thoughts he needed right now. He needed to think positively, and enjoy what time he had left with his daughters.

Before he could return home, he still had a little work to do.

It was a fifteen-minute drive to Cain's house. He didn't bother with the front door, but went around to the back door that led to the dark room. It was more of a conference room that came out of some crime drama TV show.

It was standard among all the guys not to use the front door. It was considered an interruption on Cain and Nora's personal life, and they tried very hard to keep work and life separate. Although, considering the past year almost two years, they had failed miserably at it.

It wasn't all bad. Several of the guys found their mates. Despite the dangers they faced, everything always turned out fine.

While the guys had always been close, they were like family more than ever, now. Cain and Nora had their son Ashton; Harper and

Marshall had their baby, Vince; and Andi was recently married to Samia with her cute daughter, Maisah. Family cookouts and play dates were so normal in their lives; it was as if each child had several sets of parents.

The set up they had was wonderful. It gave AnnaLee more days off, and Sam enjoyed seeing all of his friends. Unfortunately, they all had their happy endings and Sam wasn't so sure he would get his.

He had practically thrown away his faith in the mating bond, after his marriage to Jordan. The only girls he needed in his life now were Emma and Jose. At least that's what he told himself.

Sitting in the dark room, Sam wondered why he was even there. He hadn't told Cain about the re-evaluation. The only person he had talked to about Jordan was Andi, and while the boy could be a bit of a clown, he was surprisingly good at keeping his mouth sealed.

As the thought to leave was about to become more of a reality, Cain walked in.

"I thought I heard the door," Cain said.

Sam looked at him, and knew Cain instantly recognized the exhaustion and haphazardness written in Sam's expression. Cain went rigid, and slipped his hands into his pockets. He was ready for whatever Sam had to say, but Sam wasn't even sure if he was ready.

"What's up?" Cain asked.

"Take me off any upcoming missions. For at least the next six months."

Cain's jaw slackened, but he worked it together, and kept it closed. He waited for Sam to continue, but Sam wasn't going to offer up information freely. He rarely did.

"Why?" The question finally came.

The look Sam gave Cain was withering. It hurt to think about it, let alone say it. He knew he would have to eventually, but did it have to be today?

"What do you need?" Cain changed his question.

"I need to be taken off any missions."

Sam had never fought with Cain, but he thought he might be

willing to. He was wound up enough. He rolled his shoulders and neck, trying to loosen the tension.

Cain shook his head. He wasn't going to remove Sam from anything.

"Why are you here, Sam?"

"I don't know. I should have gone to Andi's."

A hint of hurt flashed through Cain's eyes. "You'll talk to Andi, but you won't talk to me?"

Cain had a right to be hurt. He'd started the group of PI dragons, and had personally recruited every member. Cain had a personal history with each one of the guys, and for Sam to choose Andi over Cain was like flushing that history down the drain.

"I won't have to say anything. I've already talked to him." Sam heard his voice crack and quickly turned his head away.

Cain pressed his lips together and nodded his head. "Go see Andi then. It's clear he'll be helpful."

Sam wasn't really sure Andi would be helpful, though. Sure, he didn't need to talk to Andi, if he just needed to talk. Maybe that was exactly what he should do, which is why he didn't want to do it.

His head was spinning.

"I'm giving the girls to their mother."

Sam spoke to the door. He couldn't bear to look at Cain. The atmosphere in the room froze.

For the third time, Cain asked, "Why?"

"I'm never home Cain. Hell, I came here from the courthouse, and I should have gone home."

"Then go home," Cain said.

There was tenseness in his voice. Cain was protective of family values, and Sam was breaking one of the most important rules. He was putting himself before his family.

"I can't," Sam's voice cracked again, and this time he didn't bother to hide his face. He looked at Cain, and let the single tear slip from the corner of his eye into the corner of his pressed lips.

Cain took a deep breath and raked his fingers through his hair. He motioned toward the table, and then left the room, going into the house. When he returned he brought in two steaming cups of coffee.

They sat there, staring into the black and bitter abyss in their cups, taking slow, desperate sips. Maybe the caffeine would present itself as a good excuse for Sam's racing heart.

Sam didn't say anything, but gave Cain a pat on the shoulder before he left.

"I'll pick up my car tomorrow."

He was hardly out the door when he shifted and climbed into the skies.

The morning had started brightly, but by late afternoon, the sun was already setting the sky into bright flames of gold and amber hues. The evenings were more and more beautiful as the nights grew longer.

His dragon lungs pulled in a draught of fresh air. He held his breath enjoying the oxygen seeping into his bloodstream and the pain in his lungs straining to ration what was left until he took another breath. Sam burst through a large cloud, feeling its misty composition breaking upon his scales. His beating wings stilled the beating of his heart.

When he landed, it was in Andi's yard. Andi was outside cooking on the grill, Maisah was in the sand box, and Samia was just walking outside when Sam landed.

He shifted, and Andi gave him one look over before handing the spatula to Samia to finish the burgers.

Sam followed Andi into the kitchen. Andi pulled out a beer and tossed it to Sam.

After a quick swig from the bottle, Sam said, "I saw Jordan today."

It was just as hard to say as he thought it would be.

"Shit, that was today," Andi said.

Sam nodded.

"Wanna stay for dinner?"

He should say no. He should go home and eat with his daughters, but his mouth and tongue were already saying "Yes," before any family values could convict him.

The girls were with AnnaLee. He comforted himself knowing that AnnaLee was there. She was always there at a moment's notice, ready to help with anything.

And he had snapped at her that morning.

He couldn't do anything right, could he?

"How does one go about apologizing to a babysitter?" Sam asked, as he and Andi walked back out onto the porch.

"Depends," Samia began, "what did you do?" She was dressed nicely in a pair of stretch capris and large sweater despite the hot weather, although, compared to Algeria, it wasn't nearly as hot as she was probably used to.

"I yelled at her for making me late. She's never been late before, and the one time she is, I snapped at her. I didn't even think about what might have happened to her morning."

Samia placed a hand on her hip while she flipped the burgers on the grill. Andi said Samia loved cooking and was a natural at it. They constantly ate a mix of American and Algerian foods.

"Just tell her you're sorry and maybe pay her a little extra for the trouble."

Andi nodded his head in agreement. "From what you've told me, AnnaLee's laid back. She'll accept a simple apology."

"I hope so."

Sam didn't open up about much more after that. Instead, he turned the conversation to Samia and Maisah adjusting to America, and if they had any plans for Maisah's schooling. They were looking at enrolling Maisah into an elementary school that Nora and Cain recommended.

Sam remembered looking into the same school for the twins, but in the end, he chose to homeschool them. They were incredibly smart, and he liked being able to monitor how they were learning. He and AnnaLee took a day to sit and discuss the curriculum and how they would teach the girls, while Sam was traveling.

Their choice of curriculum was a mix of several and the girls had a complete hands-on program. AnnaLee loved it just as much as the girls did, and Sam was thankful that it worked that way. Sam had to admit, he loved learning right alongside the girls in their science projects.

That was something he would miss. There would be no more messy volcanoes, attempts at cave painting, or straw and tape aqueducts. Sam wouldn't have an excuse for having butterfly houses or saying why ant farms were taking up more space on the back patio than patio furniture.

After dinner was over, Sam quickly knocked back the rest of his beer and told the family goodbye. He gave Samia and Maisah a kiss on the cheek. Andi walked out into the yard with him.

"Whatever you need, let me know." Andi rested a hand on Sam's shoulder.

"Thanks."

"Sam, I'm serious. You've always been quiet and solid support for everyone else. I don't recommend staying quiet about this."

"You want me to tell Cain?" Of course, he should tell Cain, but it was one thing to know it and another thing to be told it.

Andi shrugged his shoulders. "Have a safe flight."

Safe flight indeed. His head felt more crowded than it had earlier. Conflicting memories and emotions were battling in his mind, and he wasn't sure which side would win.

The first argument was easy enough. Tell Cain and get his experienced opinion.

The second argument was about him. It was the constant argument that never ended, the battle that never had a clear winner. This was the right thing, right?

Sam rarely lacked confidence. He made his decisions boldly and never regretted them. Regretting taking the girls was like a punch in the gut when he realized how he felt.

What was worse was that Sam couldn't tell if he was trying to justify his regret for the girls' safety or if he was being selfish and just wanted his own time back. Either way, he felt like a horrible person. He was not a great father, and for that alone, he was willing to give his daughters to their mother.

They needed a mother anyway. It would be good for all of them.

That's what he told himself to console his rising emotions.

In the air once again, Sam arched higher into the sky. He wanted to catch the cold air and feel it whip his face as he dipped and dived back down. The moon was a bright satellite, helping clear the fuzz that disrupted his mind.

Whatever happened, whatever the truth was about how he felt, spending time with his girls was the most important thing, now. He wanted to give them the best time ever, so when they were with their mother they wouldn't forget about him. He wanted them always to remember his love for them.

His house was only a block away from Andi's, but he took his time circling the whole neighborhood several times. When he finally landed, it was quickly becoming late. All of the lights in the house were off. Sam had to use a key to enter.

AnnaLee was always cautious, and he was thankful for that. Flying or driving, Sam made sure to have a house key on him, because AnnaLee always made sure she locked the house when it got late.

The first thing Sam did was go upstairs to look in on his daughters. They were curled around their dearest stuffed animals, with the softest smiles on their faces. Sam had never known anyone to smile while they slept, but his daughters did every night.

He walked down the hall to the spare room that had quickly been dubbed AnnaLee's room. He knocked on the door, but got no response. She was either asleep, or she was in his library.

Back on the first floor, he walked to the back of the house. The library was barely larger than a closet. It was probably designed to be an office, but with no windows, Sam knew he would never work there.

What he could do in that room was hide. AnnaLee seemed to think the same thing.

The only warning he gave before walking in was a light rap of his knuckles above the doorknob.

AnnaLee was wrapped in the softest blanket in the house, her feet curled under her, and a blue paperback in her palms. Her light brown hair was swept over a shoulder, well out of the way of the book, and her lashes glistened with unshed tears. Sam hoped she was crying over the book, and not over whatever happened to her that morning, but something in him told him he was wrong.

She seemed to have had a bad morning, and he had yelled at her. He could see it in the curve of her shoulders, the way her eyes lifted to his face and flickered with caution.

She stood up quickly, nearly tripping on the blanket that had been tucked under her feet. "You're home," she said. Her bottom lip was swollen from biting it all day.

"Yes," Sam said. "And I need to talk to you." He didn't wait to see if she would follow, but walked to the kitchen.

He would need coffee for this.

He walked in and out so abruptly, AnnaLee wondered if she had fallen asleep and dreamt of Sam returning. He had stood in the doorway, looking as if he was not at all surprised she was there, but also pained to find her still awake.

To say she remembered what happened in the morning was an understatement; it was all she had been thinking about, since putting the girls to bed, and seeing Sam now, she had to keep herself from reaching up and wiping away the tears that she knew had settled onto her cheeks. She watched as his eyes flickered over her face, and he took her tears to mean she was hurt by what he had said.

If only he knew, it had nothing to do with him.

She stumbled out of her blanket and tripped after him toward the kitchen. When she walked in, she could hear the pot of coffee brewing. She was tempted to ask for a cup for herself, but she didn't want to stay awake any longer than she needed to.

The sooner she fell asleep the sooner she could move on.

"I'm sorry I was late," she forged ahead choosing to speak first.

Despite what had happened in her morning, she should have been on time. She should have put her job first, especially Emma and Jose. The look on their faces was enough to convict her.

"What?" Sam turned slowly from the coffee pot to look at her as if she was crazy. "Why are you sorry?"

"I was late, and I should have been on time. I promise it will never happen again." She folded her arms around herself and tried to shrink away from his gaze.

"I don't care," he said. His voice fell flat. "You could be late every day for the rest of the time you're with us, I don't care."

Now she was confused. This morning he had cared a lot about her being late. The slamming door echoing through her memory told her as much.

"But—"

"I was an ass, and I'm sorry," he said.

AnnaLee straightened up and pursed her lips. "Yeah, you were," she said.

The coffee machine dripped the last drop of black into the pot, filling the silence between them. Sam's face filtered through responses, not prepared for AnnaLee's confirmation. AnnaLee bowed her back and tucked her shoulders around herself again.

"I'm sorry," Sam said, realizing there wasn't anything left for him to say or a reason to defend him.

"I know, and I forgive you." She loosed a dry laugh. "Hopefully, I'm not late again."

He smiled wanly, before he turned and poured the coffee into two mugs. Sliding one cup towards her, he said, "Thank you."

She held the warm cup between her hands, allowing it to replace the blanket. She knew he was being honest, but a part of her was upset that they weren't fighting. She could feel the pent up emotions raging for a fight.

"Thank you," he said. "If you want to talk about what happened. . ." He trailed off, letting her supply the missing words.

"I don't," she said.

But, she did. Some part of her felt this pull on her tongue to tell him everything that had happened. She didn't know what it was, but Sam always had a way of pulling truths from her, of getting her to speak what was on her mind or to laugh.

She looked up from her cup, and watched as Sam stared into the black liquid that swirled in his cup, waiting for her reply. When he looked up and met her eyes, it felt as if a spark shocked through the air, creating what seemed to be a resounding pop that could be heard echoing through the house. She jumped from the surprise and sent the black coffee spilling over the shattered mug.

She jumped back, trying to avoid the hot coffee and the spilt china. "I'm so sorry!" she cried, as she got to her knees and began to reach for the cup's shards.

"No, stop. I don't want you to cut yourself." Sam was around the island counter and kneeling next to her in a heartbeat.

He pressed a towel to the coffee, and reached to take the shards from her hand. As their fingers touched, an electric current swam through her fingers again. She gasped and pulled her hand back, falling away from Sam.

"I'm sorry," AnnaLee said out of habit. She watched as Sam froze, flexing his hand. It was obvious he felt it too, whatever *it* was.

Catching himself, Sam picked up the rest of the broken china, and set it onto the coffee soaked towel. "Don't be," he said.

He cleaned up the rest of the mess, depositing it all in the sink. When he came back around her to her, she was still sitting on the floor, her knees drawn close to her chest. "Would you like help getting up?" he asked, clearly thinking about their hands touching again.

It was a good question, she realized. She had just freaked out, and she wasn't sure she wanted to again. However, she also wasn't sure her legs would be able to hold her.

She gulped down the anxiety, which was heavy in her mouth, and held out her hand. "Sure," she said.

He pulled her to her feet, his hand a hot poker in hers. He helped her onto the stool at the counter and sat down next to her. "Should I make you another cup?"

It was clear this was just as strange for him as it was for her.

She shook her head. "No. I need to be able to sleep tonight."

The idea of sleep seemed to strike him across the face, as he whipped his head to his own cup and frowned at it, as if it had somehow betrayed him.

"Right," he said. "I forgot about that."

AnnaLee laughed. "You forgot about sleep?"

Suddenly, she was relaxed again. His presence was comforting, as it always was. Whatever had happened was strange, but they were both tired.

She slumped forward in her chair, folding her arms onto the counter to rest her head upon it. "Where did you go today, Sam?"

At first, she wasn't sure he heard her. Then, she wasn't sure he understood her when said, "Beyond the clouds across the moon."

Whatever he meant by that sent chills skipping across her skin. It was as if a key had been inserted into an unknown lock in her heart, and suddenly she wanted to know what that was like. How could she go beyond the clouds and across the moon?

Sam shook his head slowly. "I had an appointment with my ex-wife today."

The peace that had settled like a warm cloak over AnnaLee, lulling her to sleep, was ripped from her. A sense of danger crept through her mind like a prowling lion, looking for the trap.

"Why?" The question was a lot breathier than she intended, betraying her feelings. She didn't know why she cared, but she did.

He shook his head again. "You're tired. We can talk tomorrow."

She looked at the clock above the sink, and saw that it was almost midnight. Where had the time gone? Sitting up, she felt her body protest and wondered how long she had been slouched there staring at him.

"Should I drive you home, or would you like to stay here tonight?"

AnnaLee waved her hand. "I've got everything here."

She stretched her hands above her head and slowly stood to her feet. She looked at Sam for a moment, watching his eyes follow her movements and, on an impulse, she hugged him. Her arms wrapped around his shoulders, and she lightly patted his back.

"You can always talk to me," she said.

His entire body went rigid, but after a few seconds, he relaxed and returned the hug. He rubbed slow circles on her back, keeping close to her shoulders. "You too," he said.

Pulling away, she said goodnight and moved upstairs.

She hadn't realized how exhausted she was until she collapsed on her bed. She didn't even bother changing out of her clothes. She should grab her little travel bag from the dresser and go to the bathroom she shared with the girls to brush her hair and teeth, but even that sounded like too much work.

Turning to her side, she pulled a pillow against herself and curled around it.

The day had been too weird. Tomorrow needed to be better. With that hope on her mind, she drifted off to sleep.

"Mommy! Mommy!" The word was screamed from across the house. Turning around in the kitchen, her eyes saw the running form of a little girl. Her heart pounded against her chest, wild with disbelief. After what the doctor had told her, this wasn't possible, but her eyes told her otherwise. She saw a small girl with long braided hair, slide across the tiled floor until her arms were wrapped around Anna-Lee's legs.

"Mommy!" Weeping blue eyes turned upward, pleading for help.

"What is it honey?" She knelt down and used the corner of her sleeve to wipe the girl's tears.

"Sisters won't let me play with them!"

AnnaLee's heart leapt. Sisters? She had more daughters.

Coming through the kitchen were a set of twins. Tall with light hair and lighter eyes than the girl at her feet. They bore a strong resemblance to their father. Emma and Jose.

The thought jolted through AnnaLee's body so quickly that she sat up in bed and looked around. The gray paint on the walls was darker in contrast to the blue carpet that shone in the morning sun.

A dream.

Of course, it was a dream. Doctor reports like hers didn't just miraculously disappear.

AnnaLee flipped the blanket off of herself. At some point in the night, she must have crawled under it. Walking to her dresser, she quickly found the capris and blue blouse she stored in the guest room.

Grabbing her brush, she pulled it through her matted hair as she made her way to the bathroom. The girls had already brushed their teeth, leaving water and toothpaste trails on the sink. As AnnaLee washed her face, she also cleaned the sink.

She went downstairs, and walked into the kitchen to find Sam spinning maddening circles with Jose on his shoulders, and Emma laughing from a seat on the counter. When Jose spotted AnnaLee, she climbed down from her perch and ran to her wrapping her arms around her leg. The moment was so similar to her dream that it felt like a knife being twisted in her heart.

Apparently, a night's rest was not enough to move on from yesterday.

"Good morning!" Jose screamed. "Do you want to spin too?"

AnnaLee couldn't offer an answer as Jose pulled her in circles through the kitchen, not even careful to avoid Sam with Emma now on his shoulders.

"I think," AnnaLee began, sweeping Jose into her arms, "That I'm ready to eat!" AnnaLee buried her head in Jose's neck, making munching noises.

The girls were all laughs and giggles on their way to the dining room table where Sam already had a breakfast spread covering the table from one end to the next.

"Are we feeding an army?" AnnaLee asked.

"No, but I did let Cain and Nora know they could join us if they wanted," Sam said, rubbing a hand on the back of his neck.

AnnaLee looked around at the extra plates and nodded her head. She had met Cain and Nora, and their son Ashton several times, and got along well enough with them. It would be as good a distraction as anything would.

"I hope they come." AnnaLee smiled.

It was like watching a slideshow, catching glimpses of her spinning with Jose or Emma on his shoulders. She was dressed in blue, and her hair caught the morning sun that was streaming through the window over the sink. She looked as if she just walked from a garden instead of her bedroom.

As she examined the breakfast he had cooked, he watched her for any signs of what had happened yesterday. Aside from quickly covering the pain that had raced through her eyes when Jose hugged her, she was all soft smiles and genuine hope for a good day.

Sam flexed his hand at his side, remembering last night even more clearly, now that he had rested. It was something he had suspected for a while, and now he was sure of it.

AnnaLee was his mate.

In the past, he had found comfort in AnnaLee's presence. There was something about her that made him relax and trust her. The dragon inside him would often purr with delight at her presence.

Last night, he had thought his dragon would burst from him, when she dropped the coffee cup. He knew the coffee was scalding and probably hurt her feet. Not to mention, there was sharp china everywhere.

An electric current had seemed to snap into place when they looked at each other. It was the sign of an intense emotional connection; and then there was the shock that had passed between their hands, signifying a physical connection as well. It was something he never had with Jordan and had given up dreaming about altogether.

Although, even if she really was his mate, he wasn't sure it was a risk he was willing to take. If she accepted him, it would change how he moved forward with the re-evaluation, but if she refused to believe in it, nothing would change. That chance was not something he was sure he wanted to take.

The doorbell rang, pulling him from his thoughts. Cain and Nora had arrived, and Sam was grateful they would be able to buffer anything between AnnaLee and him. AnnaLee moved to get the girls into their seats while Sam answered the door.

Before he could even get the door all the way open, Ashton was already pushing through. "I'm so hungry! What did you cook?"

Sam laughed. "A little bit of everything." Looking back at Cain and Nora, he said, "I was up early."

Nora smiled. "Well I'm happy you were, because I woke up late."

"Not that you do much cooking," Cain said.

Nora hit his arm. "We split it, and today was my turn, but now I don't have to."

Sam smiled, admiring their easy banter. After closing the door behind them, he led them into the dining room, where AnnaLee was already serving up food onto the kids' plates. Each kid said, "Thanks" once she set their plate down.

Nora slipped away from Cain, and pulled AnnaLee away from the table to give her a hug. Whatever, tension had crept into AnnaLee's shoulders instantly melted at Nora's touch.

Sam always thought that was Nora's super power. She was excellent at calming women and children, which is what made her an excellent teacher. AnnaLee had similar qualities that made her an excellent nanny for Emma and Jose. Taking care of shifter children was no easy task, but no matter what came up, AnnaLee never baulked at her job and always handled every situation with grace.

Sam could count multiple times when he didn't know what to do with his own daughters and AnnaLee had had to come over and help diffuse a situation. Something about her, which Sam could now see might be the mating bond, calmed the girls and him.

AnnaLee held everyone's attention in his house. Her voice was soft and sweet like fresh marmalade. Everyone wanted to listen, let the notes of her voice ease whatever worry existed.

"Can we eat now?" Emma asked, tugging on his sleeve.

Sam placed a hand on her head. "Once everyone is seated."

Without missing a beat, Emma looked to AnnaLee and Nora and said, "AnnaLee, Miss Hollan. Can you sit, so we can eat?"

Sam clicked his tongue. "Emma."

"Please," she added with a drawl.

AnnaLee placed her hands on her hips, and looked at Emma with a frown. "No," she said. AnnaLee looked around the table, and pointed at the cups, "We don't have water."

Knowing what AnnaLee was implying, Emma hopped down from her chair and went to the kitchen to get the pitcher of water from the fridge. Sam nodded his head toward the kitchen and said, "Jose, you should help."

It wasn't long until the girls had lugged the pitcher to the table and set it next to AnnaLee. She thanked them and poured her glass before sitting. Nora, Cain, and Sam followed her.

While the adults filled their plates and started friendly conversation, the kids dug into their food. Ashton sat back in his chair, his eyes rolling to the back of his head with the first bite of French toast, and moaned. "This is so good!" he said.

Everyone laughed. Sam smiled and said, "I'm happy you like it."

AnnaLee motioned to a couple of the dishes. "Are any of these plates plant-based?" She looked up at Sam from under her lashes.

For a moment, he was swept up in her lashes, and in the color of her hazel eyes. He took a drink of his coffee to clear his throat before pointing to which dishes were plant-based. "There is vegan sausage and pancakes with oat milk."

"And are these potatoes the rest of what I bought last week?" she asked as she scooped a spoonful of the hash browns onto her plate.

"Yes," Sam said, nodding his head.

Nora leaned forward across the table to ask, "You're vegan?"

Nora and Cain were seated on one side of the table, placing Ashton at one end. Sam was seated across from Cain, next to the twins. AnnaLee sat at the head, on the other side of the girls, and next to Nora.

AnnaLee nodded her head vigorously. Plants and food were something she was very passionate about, and Sam loved being able to serve her with both.

"Yes! I've been vegan for about…" she pursed her lips as she thought about how long it had been. She turned to look at Sam.

He shrugged his shoulders. "I think you said it had been five years, a year ago, but I've the worst memory."

"That's true. So probably about six years." She turned a smiling face back to Nora.

Sam rolled his eyes, but caught Cain staring at him. Cain raised an eyebrow, and Sam's only reply was a smile. Cain's eyes widened but, respectfully, he did not say anything.

From in between them, Ashton said, "But how could you not eat chicken! It's so good!"

AnnaLee laughed. "It probably is, especially if it's fresh from a natural farm and not a meat farm; however, I prefer to let the little winged beasts live."

Cain turned his raised eyebrow on AnnaLee. "Winged beasts?"

She shrugged her shoulders. "I'm not a fan of things that can fly. They're too unpredictable."

Sam could practically hear the laughter barely contained within Cain. All Cain said was, "Interesting."

The conversation fell silent as everyone began eating, filling themselves up on carbs, protein, and sugar. The kids finished first, and were out of the dining room and into the backyard before anyone could object. AnnaLee was close behind them, wiping her mouth and setting her napkin on the table.

"I suppose I'll go after them. Can't have them wrecking my garden for the sake of an adventure."

"I'll join you," Nora said.

AnnaLee smiled, thankful for the extra assistance. Before walking out with Nora behind her, AnnaLee paused with a hand on the door. Looking at Sam, she said, "If you can clean the dining room and take the dishes to the kitchen, I'll clean the kitchen."

Sam bowed his head. "Will do."

Once they had left, and before Sam could even look back at Cain, Cain threw a towel at Sam. "You are totally whipped," Cain said.

"Is it that obvious?"

"What happened?" Cain said, standing and bracing his hands on the table. "Yesterday, you were moping in the dark room, and now you're practically glowing."

"I'm still mopey," Sam said, as if it was something to defend.

He knew Cain was right. Since being in the dark room, so much had happened. He had practically confirmed that AnnaLee was his mate, and he had never felt more hope in his life – not since the twins had been born.

"When the twins were born, I hoped they would be what saved Jordan and my marriage. It was futile to hope, but I did, and now…." He cast his eyes to the door, letting the sentence hang for Cain to fill in.

It was true though. Every time something came up and Sam would despair, AnnaLee would show up being a light of hope and salvation for him.

"What are you gonna do?" Cain asked.

"Nothing," Sam said. He stood up and began piling plates onto each other.

For now, he would do nothing. Until he had a better idea of how AnnaLee would react. He didn't want to risk losing her, not when it was about to be the most important time to have her around. With everything going on, he needed her now more than ever before.

"What?" Cain helped clear the table, stunned by Sam's answer. "Why not?"

It seemed as if it was the only question Cain knew how to ask, lately. It seemed as if Sam never had a good answer for it either.

"Is it because of Jordan?" Cain pushed forward looking for answers.

"Maybe," Sam said.

"Sam, what is going on?"

"What's going?" The dishes rattled into the sink harder than necessary. "I'm about to lose the most precious things to me, and I don't think I could stand her walking away because of magic that isn't supposed to exist."

There was the truth. And it hurt.

He rubbed his hands down his face, before bracing them against the edge of the sink. He didn't know when it had happened. He could not name a specific event, but somehow AnnaLee had inserted herself into the family. He couldn't bear to see her leave, not before he lost the girls.

His whole family, as small and disconnected as it was, would be gone before the month was out. Breathing became a labored chore.

Cain set his dishes in the sink, reaching around Sam. He pressed a hand into Sam's shoulder. "We'll figure this out."

"No," Sam said. He shook his head, and pulled away from Cain. "This isn't something for everyone to be involved in."

"You're family Sam. We're here to help."

"That might be true, but this is my family."

Although the help from everyone would probably be useful, Sam felt a strong urge to prove that he could protect what his. It was as if his dragon was waking up from a long sleep, renewed and with a purpose.

Protecting their family was the top priority for most shifters. If Sam couldn't protect his family then what was he worth? If he couldn't protect his family, why would he bother trying to protect others?

Cain seemed to sense this. He pressed his lips together and gave Sam an approving nod. "Okay."

"Thank you," Sam said.

"Whatever you need, let me know, and I'll try to get it to you."

"Thank you," Sam said again.

The back door slammed up open and feet could be heard darting through the house. "Daddy!" Jose screeched in her search for him.

"Kitchen!" He called back.

She came in gulping down air as if she had never breathed before. She complained, "AnnaLee said we can't go get ice cream, but I want ice cream."

Sam crossed his arms. "Is it only you who wants ice cream?"

She shook her head, whipping her tangled hair all around her face. "No! Emma wants ice cream, and AnnaLee wants ice cream to; she just doesn't know it, yet."

Sam laughed. "Is that right?"

She nodded her head again, looking like an over excited bobble head. Sam glanced at Cain. "You guys want to join us for ice cream?"

"While that's tempting, we promised Ashton we would take him to the museum." As if on cue, Ashton came in with Nora, AnnaLee, and Emma behind him.

"If they get ice cream, can we get ice cream?" the boy asked.

Cain smiled, "Maybe after the museum, but you don't need ice cream this early in the day."

Ashton pouted.

AnnaLee crossed her arms and said, "I agree." She stared pointedly at Sam.

"Well, I'm quite the opposite. Not only do I believe in dessert first, I think dessert should come way before dinner is even thought about." He swept Jose up into his arms, and tapped her nose.

"Right, right!" She chirped.

AnnaLee rolled her eyes before turning and giving Nora a hug. "Thank you for coming to breakfast."

Nora hugged back tightly and patted her shoulder. "Anytime you need to talk, I'm here. We're definitely friends outside of this setting."

For a minute, Sam thought he saw AnnaLee's eyes glisten. It hurt his heart to know that she was hurting, when he had no idea why.

"Thank you," AnnaLee said.

Cain ushered his family out of the house, and there was another ten minutes of goodbyes, standing in the driveway. Once they pulled away, AnnaLee was quick to turn on the girls and get them upstairs to clean up before leaving.

The way she worked with the girls was like watching a magician perform one his most complicated spells. Sam didn't know how she did it, but it was amazing and he was forever grateful.

Listening to the girls look through their clothes and move into the bathroom, he followed AnnaLee into the kitchen and watched as she rolled up her already above the wrist sleeves to just above her elbow. She dove into the dirty dishes and attacked them with the vigor of a determined woman who wanted anything but to be interrupted or distracted.

"Thank you," he said, clearly choosing to distract her.

She looked at him sideways. "For what?"

"For forgiving me, and helping me with the twins."

AnnaLee huffed. "Yeah, well at this point they're like my own daughters." A wistful look passed her eyes as she said, "I would do anything for them."

He didn't doubt it for a second.

Today. He needed to tell her today. What had happened yesterday, and what he was planning.

The trip to get ice cream went as well as could be expected with rambunctious twins, although Sam thought he and AnnaLee handled it gracefully. There were no ice cream drips on the seats of AnnaLee's car – Sam's was still parked at Cain's – and the girls were surprisingly happy with their haphazardly chosen flavors. All in all, even Sam felt he could enjoy his ice cream.

It was a relief when they got to the park. The girls were like two unleashed police dogs, enjoying a free spirited run to the monkey bars. AnnaLee rolled her eyes at their energetic display, and Sam couldn't help but laugh.

"It was nice having Nora and Cain over for breakfast. It's a bummer they couldn't have gotten ice cream with us." AnnaLee tilted her head a bit wistfully.

Sam watched her and said, "I'm happy you get along with them, but I'm also happy we have this time together." If he was going to shoot his shot, now was a good time to make his intentions clear.

She rolled her eyes at him. "Sure."

"Really, I am. We don't often get a lot of time to talk; we're so focused on the girls." He pushed his hands into his pockets while he walked alongside her.

"We should be focused on the girls now."

"I'm very focused on all of my girls," he said.

"Pfft, okay." Mirth lit her eyes. It was clear she was enjoying the banter.

He wasn't lying though. In such a public setting, his senses were always heightened toward his daughters. He knew exactly where they were and if they were talking to any of the other kids.

Just as he was aware of his daughters, he was equally aware of AnnaLee's nearness. It was hard for him not to take a deep breath to smell her. He already knew she smelt like fresh cotton and spring dew.

He had known how she smelt since the moment he met her. It was always intoxicating, and one of the first things that tipped him toward thinking she was his mate. Remembering the moment they met put a smile to his face.

"What?" AnnaLee asked, looking at him dubiously. "I'm worried to know what you're thinking about."

"Just the moment we met," he said.

"Oh, God, no. That was the most embarrassing day of my life!"

They sat down on a bench, and AnnaLee buried her face in her hands.

Sam laughed and said, "No it wasn't. You've definitely had worse."

"And you promised never to bring up that chocolate cake fiasco!"

Now Sam had an arm across his stomach as he almost keeled over with laughter.

He had met AnnaLee while she was scolding Jose in the ice cream aisle, for thinking that hiding in a freezer was a good way to play hide and seek with her daddy while he was grocery store, shopping for pull ups. Really, it just gave him a heart attack. It also found him a nanny.

Once he saw how well AnnaLee handled Jose's fit, he knew he couldn't let her go.

The embarrassing part that AnnaLee was referring to, was when she accidentally backed her car into his shortly, after they had both checked out. When she got out of the car, she was in such a rush to beg for forgiveness that she tripped; grabbing hold of Sam's heavily laden cart, and tipping it and all of its contents into the parking lot.

The chocolate cake fiasco she was referring to was another favorite moment of Sam's. She had been watching the girls for about five months, and it was Sam's birthday. Sam hated cake, but the twins loved it and convinced AnnaLee that it was the perfect cake to bake for his birthday.

The twins had pulled on their hats of trickery and convinced AnnaLee to bake the most absurd cake. When Sam came home, he found the kitchen covered in chocolate, candy, and Neapolitan ice cream. AnnaLee was on her knees with an already chocolate covered rag trying to clean up the mess.

Sam had had a horrible day at work, but the whole thing was so hilarious – AnnaLee was covered in chocolate, and the girls were practically eating the mess off the cupboards – that Sam burst out laughing. When he finally pulled himself together, he told AnnaLee to gather the girls and to take a shower. He called a cleaning service to come take care of the mess and took the three girls out to dinner.

After that night, AnnaLee had made Sam a pinky promise never to mention that day again. Sam finally straightened on the bench next to AnnaLee, taking deep breaths to control his laughter.

"You are the one who mentioned it. I was thinking of the time you thought you lost the girls."

AnnaLee pulled her eyebrows together. "I should have made you pinky promise that time too."

Sam dragged his eyes away from AnnaLee and looked to the playground where the girls were playing on the pirate ship. "They'll always be the best hide and seek players."

AnnaLee tilted her head. "You say that as if you'll never play it with them again."

There it was. He supposed he couldn't put it off any longer. Now was as good a time as any to tell her.

"I might not in a few weeks."

AnnaLee's whole body went rigid. "What do you mean?"

"I met with a court attorney and their mom, yesterday. We're going to do a custody re-evaluation."

Sam finally looked back at AnnaLee, and the dragon within him raged.

When it came to AnnaLee, his dragon had always been quiet. There were little nudges and slight aches when they were in the same house, but not the same room, and there was always a pain when it seemed she was sad, but not rage.

At that moment, AnnaLee looked as if she had been shot in the heart. Her face was suddenly pale and her hands were shaking. She opened and closed her mouth several times before she decided on one word, "Why?"

Her voice was barely a whisper, and Sam wished he could take it all back, but even if he chose not to tell her, it wouldn't change the circumstance.

"I'm never home. The girls need consistency, and I can't provide that for them."

"So you're just going to get rid of them?" Her voice shook on every word.

"They'll go to their mother."

"Who has never wanted to see them, before." Anger seeped through every word. "And what about me?"

He had thought about that. He thought this would be good for her. Give her more time to herself.

He was about to say as much when she held up her hand and said, "I want to go home."

"AnnaLee—"

She was already getting up from the bench and calling for Emma and Jose.

"Anna—"

"No." She turned around so sharply. "No, I don't want you to talk right now."

Her eyebrows were pulled together. It was clear she was hurt and confused, and nothing he said would make her better.

His dragon roared in him, pushing against his rib cage, wanting out to fight the enemy that didn't exist.

No. He was the enemy.

He had hurt her.

Emma and Jose were holding AnnaLee's hands.

"Sam, take us home."

Like a robot set to respond to her voice and her voice alone, he stood and moved to the car. Once everyone was buckled safely in their seats, he drove home. He didn't look at her, but kept his face toward the window, trying to think of the countless ways he could save her from himself and what he had said.

The day had started so well. Everything was perfect.

Now it was not.

Custody re-evaluation? What in the world was Sam thinking? These girls were his world, and the moment they were gone, he would deteriorate into nothing.

She could see it like a movie before her eyes. "The Downfall" is what it would be titled. It would be a tragic story of a stupid father and an even stupider nanny.

To think that Nora had been teasing her after breakfast about how much she and Sam acted like a couple. They were standing on the back patio watching the kids play. Ashton had been exasperated with the twins, but was letting them hang with him anyway.

"So you and Sam," Nora said, nudging AnnaLee with her elbow.

"Oh my God, please don't continue that sentence."

"What? I'm not saying anything." Nora waggled her eyebrows.

"Uh-huh, sure you're not."

Nora had laughed and dropped the subject after saying, "You do function really well as their mother. Anyone would think they belonged to you and you belonged to him."

"Except we are not possessions, Nora."

Nora shrugged her shoulders and kept her mouth shut.

AnnaLee would be lying if she said she hadn't thought about it before, though. She and Sam worked around each other seamlessly when they watched the girls together. It was natural, as if it had always been that way.

On more than one occasion, she had let her mind wander; thinking about what it would be like to belong to Sam. He would treat her delicately with intelligent conversations and feather-light touches that would leave goosebumps all along her flesh. The more the image evolved in her mind, the more she squirmed.

God, she even let herself dream of the girls being her daughters. She was willing to come to terms with her being unable to bear children, as long as Emma and Jose were around. Now, even that was being taken from her. Just when she thought she was standing on stable ground, everything rocked violently like a ship in a storm. She was reminded how much she was not in control – just along for the ride.

The car ride to the house was painfully quiet. Even the girls remained silent in the back.

Once the car was parked, AnnaLee was out of her seat and helping the girls out of the car and into the house. She pushed them toward the stairs to go play in their rooms. They lingered on the steps and watched anxiously as Sam came in.

"It's all right; your dad and I just need to talk in private." She hoped her smile was convincing enough – hoped they really did have nothing to worry about.

They nodded their heads and disappeared.

"AnnaLee," Sam said her name as if he was the one in pain.

"I need a glass of water."

Avoiding contact with him, she moved quickly into the kitchen. She filled her glass and drank it slowly. When it was empty, she filled it again.

"Can we talk?" he asked.

The answer was a clear no. She kept chugging water as if it would clear the problem like it was supposed to do for skin.

"AnnaLee, please believe me when I say I'm doing this in everyone's best interests."

She slammed her cup down on the counter.

Best interests? That was the dumbest thing she'd ever heard. He was doing this because he was scared. She glared at him and watched as he flinched from her stare.

He made to step toward her, and opened his mouth to say something else, as if he could fix the situation. Before he could move; before he could even utter a word, AnnaLee gasped and quickly pressed a hand to her abdomen.

What a perfect time for fibroid pain. It came in waves and she could usually ignore it, but this was strong, probably from her high hormones because she was angry. She bit down on her bottom lip and closed her eyes.

"AnnaLee, what's wrong?" He actually sounded concerned, although she couldn't imagine it being sincere. Besides, what kind of question was that? The only thing wrong was the fact that he was giving up his family, all for a little fear.

Suddenly she felt his arms wrap around her. She wanted to push him off, but another spike of pain lanced through her pelvic region. Blinding light shattered her vision.

She wanted to cry. Maybe she already was. Maybe there was a lot wrong, if he was carrying her to the living room. Dammit. Her knees had given out on her.

She finally opened her eyes, after he had set her on the couch. His face was swimming with concern. He cupped her face and wiped the tears from her cheeks with the pad of his thumbs.

"Please, tell me what's wrong. What happened? Why are you in pain?"

He spit-fired his questions; not even giving her space to answer.

She pushed herself up to a sitting position. She laid a hand on his shoulder meaning to push him away, but only managed to draw him closer.

"Why?" she gasped. Now she was crying and loudly. There was even snot dripping down her nose. She hated that she looked like this in front of Sam, but there was nothing else she could do. Everything hurt. Her pelvic area hurt; her heart hurt.

"AnnaLee—"

Again, she didn't give him room to finish before she said, "I can't even have kids, and you're going to take the only ones I have and give them to some woman who doesn't care!"

"I can't be with Emma and Jose all the time. The truth is I'm not a consistent parent for them."

"And what am I?"

She was the nanny. Of course. That's all she was ever supposed to be. Disposable.

"You are not disposable," he said. She must have said that out loud. Sam shook his head and continued, "You are more important to those girls than chocolate candy ice cream cake."

"And I'll become nothing to them if you get rid of them."

He sighed and put his head down. He was holding her hand. She didn't even remember him grabbing it, and she didn't pull away from him. She was surprised at the connection, and the warmth it provided her. It coursed through her and distracted her from the physical pain.

"I can't have babies," she said. She didn't know why she cared to admit that to him. "I can't have babies, because I have fibroids in my uterus, and the girls whom I've helped to raise over the past year – almost two years – are going to be gone in less than a month."

She slipped her hand from his, and looked at his shocked eyes. His face that said he wanted to fix things but he didn't know how. "And you don't even care."

That was the biggest lie she'd ever said, and unfortunately, she believed it. It hurt to believe it, but she did.

"How can I explain that it's better for everyone?"

"You can't, because it's only better for you."

She pushed off the couch, ignoring the pain that now consumed every inch of her and stumbled to the door. She had to leave. She couldn't be with him anymore. His nearness was muddling her mind, and she didn't want to be muddled.

She almost hated that he didn't follow her, but she was also thankful he respected both of them enough not to. There was nothing he could say to make her better, and he wasn't about to stop the re-evaluation, even if she begged, and the thought had crossed her mind.

It took a couple of minutes for her breathing to even out, and for the pain to subside enough for her to be able to drive reasonably well. As she pulled out of the driveway, she looked up at the house, and another ache, a different ache, pulled in her stomach. She had told the girls everything would be alright, and she had been horribly wrong.

This would probably be the last time she would see them for a while, and she hadn't even gotten to say goodbye. However, out of spite and out of love for them, she wouldn't be coming back, to force Sam to spend as much time with them as he could. If he was willingly going to give them up, then he could at least give the girls the courtesy of spending the rest of their shared days together.

With one last glance at the girls' windows and at the door, AnnaLee pulled away from the house. She blinked away the threatening tears and made her way to her parent's house. She parked outside of the little house. It looked as if it came from a story book. A red-painted door and a white picket fence dressed the house nicely.

As she walked up the drive, she could see her mom in the kitchen, busying herself with prepping dinner. Even though it was only Anna-Lee's dad and her, she still made large meals and gave leftovers to people from her church. Of all the people in the world, AnnaLee's mom was the sweetest, most genuine woman to walk the earth.

"Mommy?" she called stepping into the house. She kicked her shoes off at the carpet, and bit her lip to keep pushing the tears back.

"AnnaLee? What are you doing here?" She came into the mud room, wiping her flour-dusted hands on her apron.

AnnaLee looked up and she started crying as soon as she saw her mom's face. Her shoulders shook with a hurricane force, and she felt her heart wilt. She dashed into her mothers arms and hugged her tightly, as if that would keep her together.

Somehow she ended up in the kitchen snapping beans while her mother peeled potatoes.

"And you just left them?" her mother asked, glancing up from the potatoes, but not slowing her peeling.

"What else was I supposed to do? I felt as if I was going to break in two, and I couldn't let the girls see that."

"No, instead you let them see you run away from the problem. That's a much better example."

"Mom," AnnaLee whined.

"And what's this with warmth and tingles in your hand? Huh? Do you like him?"

"Mom!" AnnaLee dropped the beans and covered her face with her hands.

"Well, do you?"

"I don't know. Maybe, yes."

She had never asked herself the question so plainly. She had always allowed herself to daydream about the possibility of a relationship with Sam. Since he returned from Algeria, her dreams had even taken an unexpected turn that made her cheeks turn red.

Truthfully, there was a lot that changed when Sam went to Algeria. The day he left, AnnaLee had begun to have restless nights. She thought she would never sleep soundly again, until he returned and the dreams started.

"AnnaLee, you're blushing. Now be honest, do you like him?" Her mom pointed a half peeled potato at her.

Picking up the beans again, AnnaLee snapped a few and mumbled, "Yes, I think I do."

Her mom sighed and was silent for a moment. "Then I'm sorry. I'm sorry you're losing all your children in one go."

The tears began to well up again, and AnnaLee struggled not to cry into the beans. The babies in her dreams were gone, and the twins, who had stolen her heart, were about to be gone as well.

She told herself she was foolish for feeling so hurt. She wasn't their mother, so she shouldn't have allowed herself to get so comfortable. She was the nanny, and it should have been left at that. She tried to convince herself of that now, but there was no denying how she felt and what she had hoped for. There was no getting over it right away. It would take time.

She and her mother worked in silence for the rest of the afternoon, and AnnaLee skipped dinner altogether, not feeling hungry. It was too early to go to bed, but she curled up against her pillows anyway. Without even trying to keep herself awake, she drifted off to sleep.

Sleep was just as painful as staying awake. Tossing and turning, pulling herself out of the dreams that plagued her, it seemed as if even her subconscious wanted her to go back to Sam and the girls. They could figure things out; life didn't have to be so disastrous.

That's what the Sam in her dreams whispered to her. The brush of his lips against her ears and the hot breath from his whispers sent chills along her skin. His fingers played with the hem of her shirt, swiping across the slivers of skin that he exposed by pushing upwards, bit by bit.

Her hands traveled to his waist and settled on the top of his jeans. She leaned into him, allowing every hard edge of him to support every soft curve that made up who she was.

A finger tilted her face up towards him, and he allowed his lips to drag lightly across her cheeks, until they almost met her lips. "Anna-Lee," he whispered against her skin as if it was the name of an angel to be revered.

The top sheet was drenched in sweat. She sat up and kicked it off, before the dream could continue. She had already stripped off her other clothes from earlier, similar dreams.

Everything was hot and soaked for a million different reasons.

She liked him.

She was mad at him.

She needed to be near him.

Those girls were as much hers as they were his, so how dare he threaten to get rid of them.

She fell back into the pile of pillows, accepting that her thoughts and body weren't going to stop betraying her for a long while. She let each excited nerve and each anxious thought have their way, moving her hands over her own body, trying to self soothe and self satisfy the aches that pulsed within her.

It would take time was the last thing she thought, as release lanced through her body, pulling her to the brink of exhaustion, and into a mindless, blank sleep.

SAM

"How does Thursday sound?"

Michael Thurshin had called to set up the re-evaluation. For some reason, Sam had thought that it might not happen. He had somehow convinced himself that Thurshin would forget or didn't care, and the whole thing would never happen.

He was wrong.

"This Thursday?" Four days from now Thursday? Sam wanted puke.

"Yes, this Thursday," Thurshin said.

He was bored, Sam thought.

"Uh, sure. I guess." It wasn't as if he had much of a choice anyway.

"Excellent, and any one who is heavily involved in the girls' lives should be there."

"What do you mean?" Wow. Today was the day to play dumb.

Thurshin sighed, knowing that Sam was stalling the inevitable, refusing to believe that losing his daughters was an actual possibility. "If there are any babysitters or a nanny who the girls might have imprinted on, it'll be good if they are there."

So AnnaLee. AnnaLee needed to be at the evaluation. That was going to be a more difficult task than the whole evaluation.

51

"Oh, yeah, sure." Sam was in a daze and was fairly convinced the whole thing wasn't real.

"See you Thursday Mr. Lorin." Thurshin didn't even wait for Sam to say goodbye. The phone clicked and it was over.

Too easy. Too simple. Sam was going to be sick.

What he should have done was call AnnaLee right away and be done with the pain of the conversation, but he didn't.

Sam spent as much time with Emma and Jose as he could. He set up as many playdates and father-daughter dates with them as he could. He didn't want to miss one second. He even bought a camera and several memory cards to fill with pictures of the girls. This was something he should have done ages ago. He had pictures on his phone, but had never been so desperate, so avid, to get pictures to remember.

He surprised himself with these moments with Emma and Jose being some of the best that they had ever had together. He wished he hadn't waited until the last minute to treat them with such devotion. It was further proof that they deserved more.

Wednesday night, after he had settled the girls in for one more movie before bed, Sam convinced himself to call AnnaLee. The girls had been asking about her, and Thurshin had practically demanded she be at the evaluation tomorrow.

His thumb hovered over the call button.

Since she had been gone, he had gotten little to no sleep. The feel of her hand in his hand haunted him, and he often clung to the wisps of memory of her voice, to calm him down when he felt anxiety or panic rising within him. His dragon had been restless, and Sam barely kept it from ripping out at an inopportune time, when something reminded it of AnnaLee.

Those moments had Sam dissociating. His chest would get tight and he would lose sense of where he was or what he was doing. Even now, with his thumb hovering over the call button, he could feel his chest getting tight.

Suddenly the phone started buzzing in his hand. Coincidentally, AnnaLee was calling him. Just seeing her caller ID stole his breath away. Before he could answer the call, she hung up. Not even a minute later and she was calling him again.

"Hello?" He answered it quickly.

"Sam?" She sighed. "Of course it's you. I called your number."

"Is everything okay?"

AnnaLee rarely called him. When she did call, it was because she needed help with the girls.

"It's stupid," she mumbled.

"What is it? Is something wrong?" He wished they were face-to-face.

He wanted to see her expression, reach out and hold her hand. It was hard, nearly impossible, to comfort her over the phone. If something was wrong, he didn't know what he would do.

He didn't even know where she lived.

"No, nothing's wrong."

"AnnaLee, you're killing me." He raked a hand through his hair.

She was silent for a minute, dragging out the moment.

"Did you buy groceries?" she blurted.

"What?"

"I' always buy the groceries, and I wanted to make sure you didn't forget. The girls do need to eat, ya know?"

Sam smiled. He was happy. His dragon was leaping with delight that she was struggling to be away from them. This was her excuse to talk to him, and to check in on the girls.

"Yes, I did buy groceries today, although I'll admit, I've been taking them out a lot."

He could practically see her rolling her eyes.

"Dinner dates are good Sam, but they need the consistency of being at home. If you take them out too much, they'll know something's wrong, and we don't want that."

We. She said 'We.' That made Sam's heart pound even more wildly.

"Sam? Sam?"

"Sorry, what did you say?"

"You're horrible. Maybe I should come over tomorrow." Her voice trailed off, clearly wanting him to say yes and to invite her.

He didn't have to invite her, though. He didn't need to come up with an excuse to call her. He had a perfectly valid reason for talking to her and it was spoiling the contents in his stomach.

"Yeah, you probably should," he said, and all the laughter gone from his voice. His body, which had loosened at the sound of her voice, went rigid again.

"Why? What's happening tomorrow?" Fear had crept into her voice, and he could do nothing but make it worse.

"Thurshin, the evaluator, is coming tomorrow and said all of the people who have an active role in the girls' life should be there."

Now he was thankful he couldn't see her. He wasn't sure he would be able to handle seeing the pain on her face. He didn't want to see her whole body shaking with something he couldn't prevent or fully understand.

"And you didn't think of telling me this earlier?"

"I couldn't, AnnaLee." His voice cracked, and he hated himself.

The silence that hung between them was deafening. It was dissociating. Sam couldn't remember if they had hung up or if she was still there.

He needed her to be there still, but he dreaded it if she was.

"What time?" she croaked. She was crying.

He could imagine her face, with tears streaming down her cheeks, slipping into the corner of her mouth and choking her. He hated that he could see the image so clearly.

"Can you be here at nine?"

"Sure."

She didn't even say goodbye. The dial tone rang in his ear like the sound of a final execution. The blade was whistling through the air coming for his exposed neck.

He put the phone in his pocket and returned to the girls. They were already passed out on the couch. He would let them sleep there, if only so he didn't need to go through the night alone.

It didn't matter though. His dreams were still haunted.

AnnaLee was crying in his dream, and he kissed away every tear. He kissed her eyes, and before the next tear could fall he caught them up in his lips. Following their trail, he kissed down to her mouth, until he felt her press into him.

It was slow and careful. He wanted to comfort her. He wanted to show her that he was there for her and would never give her another reason to cry, because she was crying because of him. Slow and careful, he repeated to himself.

But, maybe she was comforting him. She pressed harder and ran her tongue along the seam of his lips. They became crashing tongues and tides pulling each other closer and deeper. In all the right places he was hard and she was soft. His hands were tangled in her hair, and her hands were tangled in his shirt.

But this was a dream. They didn't need clothes. Sam jerked awake. Even in a dream, he would not take advantage of her.

He rubbed his hands over his eyes and checked the time on his phone. It was seven in the morning – time for his first cup of coffee. He should have woken up earlier, so he could have started drinking coffee earlier. As it was, he couldn't get enough in his system. The morning was going about as well as it did when he went to meet Jordan to set up the re-evaluation.

It was a nightmare, however, instead of the girls being rambunctious or AnnaLee being late, the girls were cranky, and Sam couldn't get ahold of AnnaLee to ask her to come earlier.

Sam had never seen the girls so riled. They were acting like a real pair of fledglings. He was horrified to think of what would happen during the re-evaluation if he couldn't get them to calm down. Emma and Jose were screaming and throwing anything and everything at the walls. They were pulling each others hair and trying to bite whatever they could. Sam almost wondered if they were teething dragons, but it was way too early for that.

A young dragon didn't begin to grow fully its form until puberty. The girls were still in preschool.

Sam wrestled Emma away from the table, before she decided to climb across and steal Jose's breakfast. Jose was already beginning to squeeze the pancakes between her little fists when he heard the door open. He prayed that it wasn't Thurshin, but he also didn't want AnnaLee to see them like this.

He held Emma closely as she broke down in tears, asking why Jose had pancakes and she didn't (because she threw her pancakes at the wall already). He walked out to find AnnaLee frowning at the mess in the kitchen.

"What is going on?" Her voice was tense, and she looked completely unfazed.

"I don't know," Sam said, rubbing circles on Emma's back.

"What did you do?" AnnaLee accused as she took Emma into her arms so he could pick up Jose, who was crying in the doorway to the dining room.

"I did nothing!" he said. It was a horrible defense, but it was all he had.

"This is not going to help you with the evaluator," she hissed, trying to keep her voice low to keep the girls calm.

"I know that, so help me fix this. Thurshin will be here in about an hour."

"This is not an hour fix, Sam! This is an all day ordeal."

"You've had this problem before?" His eyes were wide, wondering how he had never known about this. A part of him wanted this to be another reason why he needed to get rid of the girls – clearly he was incapable of helping them. On the other hand, he knew their mother would be even less capable. What did she know of fledglings and their problems?

"Tell me everything that has happened this week," AnnaLee demanded.

Sam was quick to run through every detail of the week. With everything he said, AnnaLee's face only fell more. He had screwed up big time, and he wasn't sure how.

"I just wanted to spend time with them," he said, feeling the ache of the situation deep in his chest.

"If you want to spend time with them, then don't get rid of them and be here." She took Jose from his arms and cradled both girls. She carried them upstairs to their rooms and told them to clean up as well as they could or they would get no breakfast.

Both girls slammed their doors in reply.

Turning around she pointed down the stairs to where Sam stared with his mouth hanging down to the floor.

"Clean the kitchen and dining room. If I don't stay here, then they'll throw things and fight each other again."

He didn't ask questions.

Anything that could be spilled was. Cereal was all over the counter and floor along with coffee and milk. A cup of juice had never made it to the dining room table, and then there were the actual dishes that Sam had used when he had managed to cook breakfast.

The dining room hadn't fared much better. Emma's plate was shattered into the carpet where she'd thrown it against the wall. Syrup stuck to everything.

Moving as quickly as he could, Sam had everything picked up just as Thurshin knocked on the door. At the same time, AnnaLee had the girls dressed, cleaned up, and marching down the stairs.

"Good morning, Mr. Lorin," Thurshin said.

"Good morning, please come in." Sam opened up the door, and watched Thurshin's eyes dart around the room to take in every detail. "These are my daughters, Emma and Jose, and this is their nanny, AnnaLee."

AnnaLee bent down to whisper in the girls' ears.

Emma held out her hand. "Nice to meet you, I'm Emma."

Thurshin shook her hand.

"I'm Jose," Jose said, pushing Emma to the side.

"Tss! Jose!" AnnaLee pulled Jose back.

"I'm doing what you said!" Jose yelled.

AnnaLee looked apologetically to Thurshin. "I'm sorry; they woke up on the wrong side of the bed today and will be taking an early nap." She held her hand out for Thurshin.

He shook her hand lightly and smiled. "No problem. I have nieces and nephews who can act the same way sometime."

Sam stepped closer to AnnaLee forcing their hands apart. He knew it was business, but he didn't like seeing Thurshin's hands in hers. It was one of those moments that made his dragon want to show its dominance. It was unnecessary, but Sam didn't completely disagree with it.

"Shall we move this to the living room," Sam said, holding his hand in the direction they should go.

Thurshin was quick to start asking questions. He asked several general questions about all of them, but slowly got more personal and relational. It was about forty minutes before he asked for time with Emma and Jose alone.

"Before we lose their attention completely, I would like to ask them questions without your influence on the answers," Thurshin said.

"Daddy and I will be right through the door," AnnaLee said to give them comfort.

Sam didn't like not being in there. He wanted to see what was happening and hear what the girls were saying. He tried to think through everything that could make him sound like a bad father.

AnnaLee rolled her eyes. "You're going to pace the Grand Canyon into the carpet if you keep it up. Besides, they'd have more bad things to say about me than you."

Sam winced. "That's probably not a good thing for me though," he said.

"Sorry," she said, realizing what she said implied.

"You're a great father, and he would be foolish not to see that."

Sam shoved his hands into his pocket and leaned up against the wall. "I could be a great father," he said.

AnnaLee rolled his eyes. "Sure, you've been a dick this past week, and you haven't made the best choices with the girls, but there is no doubt about the kind of father you are."

She pushed her hands behind her back and leaned against the opposite wall. There was maybe two feet in between them, and it was still too far. Sam wanted to step forward and get as close to her as he could.

"AnnaLee, last week—"

Before Sam could finish, they were rushing into the living room when Jose yelled, "No!"

Jose and Emma were on the couch playing tug-of-war with one of the six pillows. Thurshin had his hand held out, trying to diffuse the escalating fight with a calm voice. Before Sam could even say anything, AnnaLee jumped in and snatched the pillow from them both.

"Enough," AnnaLee seethed. "Jose, go pick a game and take it to your room."

AnnaLee followed Jose. While they were gone from the living room, Sam knelt down and grabbed Emma's hand. "Emma," he said, dragging her name.

Silent tears began to roll, and he pulled her in for a hug. After a minute, AnnaLee came back and took Emma to find a game for her room. Once both girls were put away, AnnaLee returned apologizing again.

"I'm sorry. It's been a really bad day for them. They haven't been told anything, and stress between Sam and I built up making them anxious."

Thurshin slowly shook his head, refusing the apology. "Really, it's okay. Kids are kids and I was asking tough questions without you being in the room."

AnnaLee offered him an apologetic smile that he couldn't refuse. "Alone, the girls should end up falling asleep. They're clearly tired."

"What about yourself? Think you're up for some questions now?" Thurshin motioned for her to take a seat on the couch.

Sam rubbed the back of his neck. "I'm guessing I'm out on this one too?"

Thurshin nodded his head.

Sam moved to the kitchen and started a pot of coffee. That was all he seemed to be drinking lately. Better a caffeine addict than an alcoholic, though. He paced the kitchen. His dragon paced right along with him. Their mate was in the other room, alone with a guy, and they could do nothing.

Sam knew Thurshin was doing his job, but he didn't like it. It seemed like forever until AnnaLee came out, and when Sam went in he was ready to fight. All of that drained from him when he took his seat on the couch.

"Nothing has changed around here, since when the girls were born," Thurshin said, leaning back in his chair and crossing his legs.

Sam nodded his head.

"Right, Sam? Nothing's changed?"

"No, Thurshin. Aside from AnnaLee and a little growing, nothing's changed."

"Then why are we doing this?"

Sam shrugged his shoulders. Why he was doing this seemed to be the most important question lately.

"Tell me you want to keep the girls, and I won't even bother going to Jordan's. We'll consider this a lapse of judgement and move on."

Sam blew out the breath he was building up in his lungs. "If it was a lapse of judgement, then we need to continue."

"Do you want to keep Emma and Jose?"

"Sure, but—"

"Yes or no, Sam. Do you want to keep Emma and Jose?"

That was the dumbest question in the world. Of course he wanted to keep his daughters.

"Yes."

"Then why all of this?"

"I'm not around, Thurshin."

"But you've got a stable girlfriend?"

"AnnaLee?" Sam pulled his head back, and looked shocked at the question. "She's just the nanny."

Thurshin shook his head again, not willing to take that as an answer. "With the way you two look at each other, I don't think so."

"Is my love life a part of the evaluation?" Sam asked, feeling his anger burn in him again.

The questions went on for close to an hour. At some point, AnnaLee poked her head in and said the girls wanted to go outside, so they could be found out there. Sam wanted to burst off the couch and follow them.

It wasn't just AnnaLee; he didn't like being separated from any of his girls for so long. When the evaluation finally ended, Sam was on his feet and shaking Thurshin's hand. Sam led him to the door, eager for him to leave.

"Sam, this is your last chance. Tell me not to, and I won't bother with Jordan. I'll call her and tell her the whole thing's off."

In his haste, Sam almost said yes, but with his hand closed around the door knob, his answer was no. "I made this choice, and we'll follow it through," Sam said.

He opened the door to let Thurshin out. As he swung it open, Jordan stood on the other side with her hand raised.

"Oh," she began, "bad time?"

ANNALEE

AnnaLee had stepped into the kitchen to get a glass of water for each of the girls. While she was reaching for the glasses she heard Sam and Thurshin talking, but what made her pause was the new voice. It was definitely female.

The female had asked if it was bad timing and AnnaLee wanted to scream through the house that it was the worst timing ever. She didn't know where this sudden burst of aggression had come from, but she didn't hate it. She felt like this was her house, with her twins, and her Sam, and sharing was not on the agenda for today or any other day.

It was already torture to have the girls questioned without her, and then Sam was evaluated the longest. She thought it would never end. The last thing AnnaLee wanted was another woman around.

"Should I be looking into things, Jordan?" Thurshin asked. By the sound of his voice, he was clearly not pleased that Jordan was here.

"Not at all. I just came to see Sam and the girls and talk about how we would move forward." AnnaLee was sure that Jordan was lying through her teeth.

By the sound of Thurshin's voice, he felt the same way. "Those types of discussions can happen through me, at the courthouse."

"Oh, but Sam doesn't mind, right?"

AnnaLee held her breath, waiting for Sam's response.

"No, of course not."

AnnaLee wanted to scream again.

"The girls are outside, so you won't see them, but you can talk to me," Sam said.

That was a little better, but AnnaLee still didn't like it.

She heard Thurshin say goodbye and then the door closed. AnnaLee wondered if Sam had stepped outside. She leaned closer to the entryway to try and hear what else would was being said.

She held the two glasses close to her chest, completely forgetting the water for the girls. She couldn't hear anything.

"AnnaLee, what on earth are you doing?"

AnnaLee jumped at the sound of Sam's voice, and she dropped both glasses. "I'm sorry!" She was instantly on her hands and knees trying to pick up the glass.

"How many times are we going to do this? Stop before you hurt yourself and let me." He knelt in front of AnnaLee and lightly pushed her shoulder to get her to back away.

"I'm sorry. I was supposed to be getting water for the girls." AnnaLee knew her face was red. She had been caught eavesdropping, and nothing she said would cover that.

"Who are you?" Jordan was still standing in the doorway. The sneer on her face could have curdled milk, but AnnaLee hardly cared; she was sure her own expression could do worse.

Sam snipped over his shoulder, "AnnaLee. Now Jordan it would be wonderful if you could help me."

Jordan pointed to AnnaLee. "You told her not to help."

"Yes, because she's AnnaLee and you are not." He said that as if it was the perfect explanation, although AnnaLee wasn't sure what he meant by it.

Jordan still didn't move to help. She crossed her arms and stared.

This was the dumbest thing, AnnaLee thought. She rolled her eyes, hardly caring to get involved in some childish stare down. Instead, she got back down on her knees to help Sam despite his protests.

They cleaned up the mess, and Sam filled two plastic cups. "I'm sorry we surprised you," he said, handing the cups to AnnaLee.

"It's okay. I'm not entirely innocent," AnnaLee said, quietly so Jordan couldn't hear.

Following her, Sam said, "Neither am I, I suppose."

Turning to face Jordan, Sam said, "AnnaLee, my ex-wife, Jordan. Jordan, my AnnaLee."

His possessive before her name did not go unnoticed by either of the women. AnnaLee felt her face flush, for completely different reasons than Jordan's face which also turned bright red. AnnaLee clearly remembered her calling Sam hers as well.

She tried to shake the thoughts from her head, but she wasn't even sure if she wanted to. A day ago, she had been pissed at Sam. She was still mad at him, but that didn't mean she wanted to be away from him. Whatever magnet they had both swallowed meant they belonged together. They were drawn to each other by the recent dilemma, AnnaLee really didn't think it was wise to resist it. Fighting the magnetism would only make things worse.

Lifting her head confidently, AnnaLee stepped closer to Sam. "Can we help you with something?"

Sam looked down, surprise written across his face when their arms brushed each other. She felt it too, the heat that moved with purpose and hope and pulled in her stomach. It was satisfying and everything she had been craving. It was as if every nightmare she had had was being washed away, and all those dreams that made her squirm in the daylight were a possibility.

If she really thought about it, which she had over the past week, there had always been something between her and Sam. His presence always relaxed her, assured her everything would be okay. The girls were a treat she could look forward to.

At some point, between losing her last boyfriend and now, she had come to consider Sam and the twins as her family. Really, how often was she home with her own family? She wasn't, because she was always in this house.

Now there was another woman threatening the family AnnaLee had come to claim.

"I want to see Emma and Jose," Jordan said, sticking her nose in the air.

AnnaLee almost laughed. Jordan was shorter than AnnaLee by several inches, and looked comical trying to act taller than her. Before Sam could say anything, AnnaLee blurted, "No."

Jordan scoffed. "Just because you're his mate, you think you have rights over the girls?"

"Jordan, enough," Sam said, his voice dangerously low.

"What?" AnnaLee asked. "His mate?"

"You don't know?" Jordan raised an eyebrow.

"I know I've been with the girls for over a year now, and have more sway with them than you ever will. They trust me, and they don't even remember your face." AnnaLee held her own, completely confused, but trying to remain confident.

"Sam, it's not like you to keep things like this from someone you like." Jordan's lips twisted into a smile.

AnnaLee didn't like being ignored. "What are you talking about? Sam what is she talking about?"

Looking at AnnaLee, Sam said, "Why don't you take the water to the girls now?"

"No. Why don't you tell me what's going on now?"

"Anna—"

"He's a dragon. A shifter actually, but he can shift into a dragon. It looks as if you're his mate." Jordan forged ahead, not caring about the impact her words were having.

"He's a magical being that shouldn't exist. One that I should have gotten rid of years ago, but allowed love to blind me so hopelessly. Have you ever seen him shift? Probably not, he's really picky about it.

But you are his mate; soulmate is what new agers call it. Pretty heavy stuff and responsibilities. If you ask me you should leave."

The silence in the kitchen was sweet. The longer AnnaLee stared at Jordan and blinked, the more Jordan's smile began to waver and slip.

Finally, AnnaLee said, "So?"

"So?" Jordan looked taken aback, not expecting AnnaLee's response. "So he didn't tell you."

"So?" AnnaLee kept her position.

"You really want to be with someone who doesn't tell you important things like that?"

AnnaLee looked at Sam, who hadn't taken his eyes off her for a moment. She could see in his eyes that what Jordan was saying was the truth, and she could see how scared he was that she would hate him for not telling her. She could also feel that it stirred a truth within her she had always known.

They were mates. It was clear as day now.

Turning back to Jordan, AnnaLee said, "He would have. Thank you, though, for ruining a moment that could have been incredibly special to us."

Before Jordan could respond, screams rang through the house.

"I'm getting my water first!"

"I'm thirstier than you!"

"Nu-uh!"

"Uh-huh!"

Emma and Jose burst into the kitchen, pulling and pushing each other, until they wrangled the cups from AnnaLee's hands. They were each half-way through gulping down their drink, when they spotted Jordan. Jordan was standing, her hands hanging limply at her side, trying to pick a facial expression, as the girls inched behind AnnaLee and Sam.

Emma tugged on AnnaLee's shirt. "Who's she?"

AnnaLee looked up at Sam, unsure how he wanted to answer. Sam said, "That's your mother."

The word made both girls cringe further and shrink behind them even more. Seeing their response, AnnaLee said, "I think you should go."

Jordan didn't argue.

Once AnnaLee was confident she was out of the driveway, she said, "Everyone in the backyard, now."

Now that Jordan was gone, her words were sinking in. Dragon. Shifter.

Impossible.

Once they were all outside, Sam spread out his hands and said, "AnnaLee, let me explain."

"Shift," AnnaLee demanded.

"What?" Sam's face looked crestfallen.

"Are the girls dragons? Is that why they have days like today?" She was still hugging the girls close to her legs, and looking at Sam, waiting for him to answer or to fly away from the pressure she was putting on him.

He shook his head. "I don't know if they are. We won't know until they're about twelve."

AnnaLee nodded her head, accepting that answer. "But we know you're a dragon, so shift."

Jose shot a hand into the air. "I want to go for a ride!"

"Me too!" Emma said, jumping with excitement.

"We can ride you?" AnnaLee said.

"It's very dangerous," Jose and Emma said in unison.

AnnaLee rolled her eyes. "Great. Now shift."

Sam took a deep breath, but he didn't try to stop anything.

In the blink of an eye, as if watching a bright light fade, Sam was gone and a beautiful amethyst dragon stood in his place. He was huge and sparkling like a girl's dream jewel.

The twins jumped up and down, clapping their hands as if it was the best show they had ever seen. AnnaLee's mouth hung open, and she couldn't say it wasn't amazing to watch or look at.

Moving forward gingerly, she reached a hand out toward the dragon, which eagerly pressed the pad of his nose against her palm. It chuffed and rolled his eyes as if saying, "Finally."

Somehow, AnnaLee felt the same way. Finally was right. She had been living her whole life for this moment.

As the realization hit her, she broke down crying. The dragon shifted so quickly, AnnaLee stumbled forward, and was caught in Sam's arms. He tried to soothe her crying, but she just cried more.

Emma and Jose looked at each other and then at Sam. "Daddy, what's wrong?"

"Nothing you did girls. Get the door for us?" Sam swept AnnaLee up into his arms and carried her into the house. Sam set AnnaLee on the couch, and both girls instantly curled up into her sides to try and comfort her.

"I'm sorry," she said.

"No, don't be sorry."

She wiped her eyes, and looked between the girls, before wrapping her arms around them and pulling them close.

"Daddy and I really need to talk about a lot of things, and we really don't want to yell in front of you. Besides, I think it's time for your nap."

AnnaLee looked pointedly at Sam. Taking her hint, Sam got the girls upstairs and settled down.

When he returned, AnnaLee was quick to ask, "Why didn't you take Thurshin's offer? Why all of this to begin with?"

"Because, AnnaLee, I really don't think I'm a good father. Because if it's possible that they're better with their mother, I want to give them that."

"You saw Jordan today! She's horrible."

"But if—"

"They're better with me, Sam! With us!"

AnnaLee could feel her chest getting tight, as the weight of the matter settled in on her. She felt the way she had after getting out of the hospital. All hope was lost.

"AnnaLee." Sam raked his fingers through his hair, and placed his hands on his hips.

"That day, I was late was because I was told I have fibroids in my uterus and can't have kids. It was okay because I already have kids, but now you're taking that away from me."

There was no stopping her crying. Her whole body shook with sobs. She covered her face, and pointlessly wiped her eyes. Sam moved onto the couch and pulled her into his arms. "I'm sorry. I knew something was wrong, and I never asked."

Hearing his gentle voice and how he carefully tried to hold her together, while her world fell apart, made her cry even more. He was perfect. Despite how he had messed up, he was perfect.

"How long have you known, Sam?" The question came out stuttered.

"About what?" He wrapped his arms around her and rested his chin on her head.

"How long have you known about the re-evaluation and that I was your mate?"

She felt him go still. The answer was too long. He had known for too long.

Her crying started again. "Why didn't you tell me?"

"I was scared that I was wrong." He took a deep breath. "Now I'm scared that I'm right."

AnnaLee pushed away from him and looked at him as if he was absurd. "You don't know if you're right?"

She couldn't believe what she was hearing. After everything that had happened, Thurshin asking questions, Jordan's attempts of accusation, seeing him as a dragon, and admitting her own feelings, she couldn't believe he didn't know if he was right.

What didn't he know? That she was his mate? That he shouldn't be giving up his daughter's because of some pathetic insecurity?

AnnaLee could answer all of those questions for him.

"What don't you know, Sam?" AnnaLee's voice was dangerously quiet. She wasn't sure if she wanted to get up and leave, or scream in his face.

"I'm not confused about anything." He grabbed her hands and held them tightly. "I know you are my mate, and I know I will do anything for this family."

She pulled her hands from his. "But you're not doing anything for this family, so maybe we're not mates." The idea of not being mates sent her into a panic. She couldn't breathe and her whole brain shut down. All her thoughts caught fire under the theory that they weren't mates.

She didn't realize she was shaking, until Sam had pulled her back into his arms and held her tighter than before.

"No, we are definitely mates."

"How do you know?"

Sam tilted her face and kissed each tear. "I know because of this." He kept kissing her tears until his lips hovered just over her lips.

"I don't know how you've been sleeping—"

"Horribly," she said.

He smiled. "Me too, except for the one dream where I do this." He slowly kissed her, angling her head up so he could comfort her better.

SAM

The dream would never come close to the reality of kissing AnnaLee. Her lips were soft, and when Sam pressed his tongue against her lips, she opened up for him, tasting sweet and fresh. As she tilted her head back, he kissed her deeper, wanting to remember the feel and the shape of her lips against his always, a perfect fit to him.

He began to kiss her jaw and down her neck to the dip of her collarbone. He could feel her fingers curling into his shirt, as he lightly nipped the pulse in her neck. She gasped at the pressure of his teeth and the insistency of his kisses.

"Better than any dream," she said. Her voice was breathy, and driving him wild.

He felt himself grow hard at the thought of her dreaming of him pleasing her. That's all he wanted to do. Please her and show her exactly how much they were mates. Unlike in the dream, he did not stop. He lifted her shirt and tossed it aside. His hands roamed up the planes of her stomach to her breasts.

Letting go of him, she reached behind herself to undo the clasps on her bra, so there would be no barrier between his slowly descending kisses and her peaked nipples. Meeting them, he greeted each pebble with a kiss, a swirl of the tongue, and a teasing pull. His hands stayed upon them, as he lowered his head down to her navel.

Eventually the button of her jeans stopped him. He looked up at her hooded eyes, seeking permission. Her hands were in his hair, and she pushed his head down.

Taking the silent permission, he undid the button and helped shimmy the jeans and panties down her legs. Once they were off, he slowly worked his way back up, kissing the arch of her feet, loving each calf, and nipping the tender flesh near her apex. Pushing her legs apart, he looked up one more time.

She squirmed underneath his gaze. She said, "Sam, please, I'm still not convinced."

He growled. He let his dragon slip out just a little, determined to show this woman just how mated they were. The moment his tongue met her button, her hips thrust off the couch. Sam held her down with an arm across her stomach, and went on pleasing her. He didn't stop, even after she had shaken and shivered beneath his strokes, he kept feasting.

"Sam," she pleaded.

Determined to bring her over the edge a second time, he did not stop. He found her tight hole and inserted a finger. Her small gasp was not enough, and he inserted two fingers, pumping them delightedly as she moaned and twisted beneath him.

After her second climax, he came up and kissed her passionately, allowing her to taste her juices all over him. To taste how sweet and beautiful she was, and how easily he knew what made her purr.

As if realizing he was still dressed, she pulled at his shirt. He grabbed her hands and held them down. He kissed her again.

"The girls will not nap forever," he said.

Desperation clouded her eyes. "Let them play in their rooms until we are done," she said.

"Who would be the bad parent then," he joked.

"Jordan, and always Jordan."

The name alone killed the mood. Sam lowered his eyes and got off of AnnaLee. He retrieved her clothes and handed them to her. "I'm sorry," Sam said.

"Sorry?" AnnaLee was taken aback. "For what?"

"For doing this at an inopportune time and not allowing us to finish."

AnnaLee stood up and took the end of the shirt Sam held out to her. "But we will finish?"

Sam stepped close to her, tilting her face up to his. "We are mates, and that was not even half of the mating process." He felt her shiver against him.

"Hurry to your room and change. I'm going to call Thurshin."

She clutched her pile of clothes to her chest and went upstairs. Sam watched her walk away, until she was out of sight.

He would be lying if he said it wasn't hard to hold himself back, but mating with her could wait, until he could promise her they wouldn't be losing their family.

"Sam, don't tell me you're calling to say you want to stop this."

"I'm calling to say I want to stop this."

The sigh that came across the phone shot down Sam's heart. He knew there was nothing that Thurshin could do. He had given Sam a one time offer, and Sam had rejected it.

"I already set a date with Jordan. Whatever happened today made her incredibly determined to win this."

"She won't," Sam said. He saw how Emma and Jose reacted toward Jordan. There was no way she was going to win.

"For your sake, Sam I hope you're right."

He fell down onto the couch and dropped his head into his hands. There was no way Jordan was psychologically sound, not after what Sam had seen today. It was clear that Jordan had thought Sam was falling apart and was upset when she saw AnnaLee. Sam would go as far as to say that Jordan was actually jealous of AnnaLee. It was stupid, but he had seen it on Jordan's face. He heard the threat in her voice, when she tried to scare AnnaLee.

But it had failed. Jordan had failed. AnnaLee wasn't afraid of him and what he was.

He was amazed at how willing AnnaLee was to accept him. She accepted what he was and what the girls could be. She had made it sound as if everything that had happened made sense, and it did.

The desire to be around each other, the pull toward each other, had a purpose. What had just happened between them was enough confirmation for him, and he hoped for her as well. As long as they could trust each other and believe in each other, mating could wait.

AnnaLee walked back into the living room. "Not good news, I'm guessing."

"He's already made the appointment with Jordan."

AnnaLee blew out a breath. "So what do we do?"

"We need to talk."

Her body went rigid and she looked at him warily. He grabbed her hand and pulled her to him, until she was sitting in his lap. He didn't want any distance between them.

"Nothing bad, baby," he said.

She relaxed, curving her back and resting her head on his shoulder. "What is it?"

"Jordan is a shifter hunter."

AnnaLee sat up straight and looked him in the eye. "What? How long have you known?"

Sam winced. AnnaLee would not like his answer, but he had to tell her the truth. "Since I've known her."

"You knew she was a shifter hunter and you were going to hand over our daughters, our dragon daughters to her!"

Sam should have been scared by how loud her voice had gotten, but all he felt was pleasure coursing through him as she called Emma and Jose her daughter, their daughters.

"There's no guarantee they are shifters," he said.

She rolled her eyes. "They are. Trust me."

"We won't know until—"

"I know! Their attitude is evidence enough. Maybe they can't shift yet, but their moods make sense."

She was right. If they weren't shifters, then they were bipolar or had something else wrong with them, and he couldn't accept that. He held her more tightly and pressed her head to his shoulder again.

"I know. The girls won't go anywhere I promise."

"Good," she said. "Did he say when he would visit Jordan?"

"No, but I'm sure we'll find out soon."

"I want this to be over already," she said. Her voice was barely a whisper.

"Me too."

"What are we supposed to do until we hear from him?"

Sam thought for a minute, dragging his fingers up and down her arm. He hoped he never got used to touching her. He wanted it to be this surreal every time he felt her skin or looked at her.

"We'll have fun with the girls."

She nodded her head, and in a sleepy voice repeated him.

He realized she must be exhausted. She had learned so much in one day and she had been the barrier between the girls going completely berserk and him losing his mind.

Already he was a horrible mate. He should have been protecting her from the onslaught of emotions and information. But she handled it beautifully.

He pressed a kiss to her forehead. She was already asleep. Lifting her up, he carried her to her room, and pulled the blanket up over her. He could have watched her sleep, but he heard the girls stirring in their rooms as he passed. She took care of them throughout the day; he could certainly step up and be a proper father for the evening.

Sam was awake the next morning, before anyone else was. He started the coffee and began breakfast, hoping to avoid the panic that his mornings had become. He didn't want to rush anything.

AnnaLee was awake shortly afterwards, and she followed her nose to the dripping coffee. "How long did I sleep?" she asked.

"You slept all through dinner last night," Sam said, making their drinks.

"And I slept in my room?" She said it like a question. Sam wasn't sure why it was a question.

He drew his eyebrows together as he handed her a cup. "Yes?" he said, slowly, just as confused as she was.

"Oh." She was quiet for a minute before she asked, "Do mates not share bedrooms? Is that a human thing?"

Sam nearly choked on his coffee. "Of course mates share bedrooms," he said.

"But I slept in my room, not yours?"

He understood her confusion now. "We didn't talk about it," he said. He wasn't about to make assumptions, now that they were mated.

She rolled her eyes. "We don't have too." He could see the laughter there, and he liked that a lot more than the pain that he had been seeing for days.

"Daddy!" Jose called as she ran down the stairs.

"No running!" he said as she slid into the kitchen. He sighed as she slowed down, once her arms were wrapped around his legs.

"I'm hungry," she said.

"We aren't eating without Emmy," AnnaLee said.

"She's not hungry," Jose countered.

Sam barked out a laugh. That was the worst lie Jose had ever come up with. Both girls were always hungry. "You mean she's still asleep," Sam said.

He scooped Jose into his arms. "Then we should probably wake her!"

A lot of laughter and another cup of coffee later, they finished breakfast, leaning back in their chairs and shoving their plates away from them.

"What are we doing today?" Emma asked.

"Nothing," Sam said. "We're staying home, relaxing, cleaning, whatever we want to do here."

He looked at AnnaLee and found her batting her lashes. "Whatever we want, huh?"

He coughed and shifted in his seat. "Within reason," he amended.
She laughed.
The rest of the day wasn't much different. The rest of the week

and well into the next week wasn't much different. AnnaLee stayed in her room, and other than a few kisses, Sam stayed well away from her. He saw the confusion and longing written on her face that he felt in his groin, as well, but he wanted to mate with her when their family was secure. He wanted it to be a promise to her.

With that constantly lingering in his mind, he kept them busy, so that he and AnnaLee couldn't be distracted. He hosted a dinner party with the rest of the dragons, inviting all the families over.

It was a lovely time for AnnaLee to meet the rest of the moms and mates in the group. He didn't want her to feel alone, and everyone was always so welcoming. AnnaLee was accepted immediately, especially thanks to Nora's endorsement of her.

While the kids played in the yard, the adults discussed ways to win the case. Although, there was nothing to guarantee Sam's winning, even with the strings they could pull. They did agree that Jordan was a wild card and needed to be watched at all times.

Before the night was out, they had a rotating schedule for each dragon to watch her house. It wasn't long until Sam and AnnaLee knew the exact moment that Thurshin went into Jordan's house and the time he came out.

The time living with Sam was like living in her dreams. That moment on the couch followed her everywhere and consumed nearly every waking thought. It felt unfinished, and simply holding his hand or pecking him on the cheek was never enough.

Nonetheless, no matter what she did, he kept his distance. He kept whispering, not yet. No matter how she dressed, after the girls went to bed, or where she slid her hands, he played the chivalrous man, no matter how dark his eyes got or the growl that built in his chest.

When she talked to the other women; the mates of the other dragons in Sam's group of friends, they all said it was normal. It was important for the men to do it at the right moment. They wanted it to be memorable. At the same time, the women said that if AnnaLee really wanted to, she could keep advancing despite Sam's nudges and comments and eventually his dragon's libido would take over.

AnnaLee did think about doing that, but she wanted to respect Sam, as much as he respected her. She even continued to sleep in her room, even though every cell in her body demanded to be near him.

She was thankful for his arms being around her when Thurshin called, after his visit with Jordan. Sam put the phone on speaker and set it on the table for both of them to listen. He kept his arms firmly around AnnaLee, holding her on his lap, and ready to keep her pieces together should Thurshin say something heartbreaking.

"Talk to me Thurshin," Sam said.

"As much as I hate to say this, Jordan checks out. Her home is clean and she's psychologically sound." Thurshin didn't sound as if it hurt him to say it.

"What does that mean for us?" Sam asked.

AnnaLee thought she would never breathe again. Absurd scenarios were running through her mind as she imagined everything that could happen. Her chest was tight, and not even Sam's reassuring presence helped her.

"It means that if this were a race between you two it would be a tie. It means I need to see her with the girls."

"No," AnnaLee said, surprising herself with how quickly and firmly she spoke. Her whole body was shaking, and she didn't feel nearly half the confidence she spoke with.

Thurshin didn't question her being there. He said, "It'll be a supervised visitation. We'll do it somewhere public."

"A park?" Sam asked.

"A park is good," Thurshin confirmed.

"No," AnnaLee said again. "The girls were petrified of her."

"I need to see that," Thurshin said. "The three of us will be there, so the girls will not be in danger." His voice wasn't comforting.

Sam asked, "Do we need to do anything before this?"

"I would talk to the twins about it. What they say and how they act will be what makes my decision for me, and they should know that."

"Alright, thanks Thurshin."

AnnaLee was grateful that Sam had spoken with Thurshin. She could hardly pay attention to the end of the conversation. Her mind was wrapped up in the awful scenarios she kept conjuring in her mind.

She squeezed her eyes closed and pressed her face into Sam's neck. She took in a deep breath of his scent and let it settle her. While she hated what they were going through, she was happy she was with him. She wouldn't give up a moment of this stress, if it meant they weren't together.

AnnaLee moved and wrapped her arms around his shoulders, trying to cling tighter to him. She knew this couldn't be easy for him.

Sam shifted her in his lap to angle her face up to look at him. "Hey, it's going to be okay."

"I know," she whispered. "When will we go to the park?"

"Saturday," he said.

Saturday was three days away. It was too soon.

"Breathe," he said. She hadn't even realized she stopped.

It felt as if the whole world had stopped. Every dream and hope she had hinged on this weekend.

"Whatever you're thinking, stop. We'll talk to the girls and everything will be fine."

He leaned down and kissed her, offering her more than the pecks he had been teasing her with. Their tongues danced, greeting each other like old friends who had forgotten what the other looked like, tasted like.

"Sam, please," she begged. "The girls are with Maisah today, and I need more. I need all of you."

"Not until our family is safe."

"If we're waiting for that then you don't believe everything will be okay."

He didn't say anything back. She had caught him in his own fear.

She moved until she could slide a hand between them and cup his already hard member in his jeans. "Please," she whispered to his lips.

"AnnaLee." His voice was rough, and he was incapable of finishing whatever he was going to say, as she kissed him.

"I'm scared, and as my mate you should help me relax."

He growled, and before she could blink, he had lifted her and laid her back on the table. She wrapped her legs around his waist and pulled him close eager for him. He kissed her passionately, ardently, branding his lips to hers.

His hands skimmed up her thighs sending sparks of pleasure

through her. Just the touch of his fingers on her skin made her crazy. Her brain was fogged every time they were together.

He reached the apex of her thighs, and she felt the tip of his fingers grazing the lining of her panties. Just the slightest touch made her gasp. His grin was feral, as he took pleasure in seeing her mouth form an O and as her eyes rolled to the back of her head, completely lost to his fingers' love.

He pushed aside her panties and dipped into her finding her slick and ready for anything he gave her. Slowly, so painfully slowly, he pumped his fingers in and out of her, using his thumb to graze over her button. The button that made her sing, every time it was teased.

"Sam, please!" she cried.

She was rising and rising, constantly on the edge of falling and he never let her, building her up until tears were streaming down her cheeks. He bent down and licked each tear, kissing her fluttering eyes.

Finally he picked up speed and ardently adored her sweet spot. Her hips jerked off the table and she cried out as she finally climaxed. It was long and almost painful, as Sam's fingers didn't stop, only slowing and dragging out the moment. Finally his thumb stilled, and he pulled his fingers out. He lifted them to his mouth, and licked them clean, before pressing pressed them to her lips. His eyes never left her face.

He pulled his fingers away from her and kissed her. "You are beautiful when you're like this."

She tried to roll her eyes. He laughed at her attempt.

"AnnaLee, I will please you anytime you ask, but I don't want us to mate completely yet. Yes, it affirms my fears, but it is also our safety net."

Fixing herself and standing up off the table, she said, "I understand that, but you don't need to deny yourself pleasure. As much as you want to give, I want to return it."

She sank to her knees and undid the button on his pants as she went. She needed to see him and taste him as much as he did her. It was unfair to keep things one-sided.

Before she had even pulled down the band of his boxer briefs she could tell he was big. He was bigger than all of her boyfriends before were, and rather than be worried, she was excited. She had her own personal dragon dick waiting for her.

Pulling down the boxer briefs completely, she took him in her hands, and marveled at the length and girth of him. She could hardly wait, and lightly pressed her lips to the tip, giving it the same peck he had been giving her.

Immediately his hands were on the back of her head, curling his finger in her hair. He was eager too, possibly more excited than she was. She wondered if he felt the same electric charge she did whenever he touched her.

Deciding he had waited long enough, she took him in her mouth, bobbing her head up and down. He moved his hips with her, at first going slow and then picking up quickly.

"AnnaLee, not too much."

She didn't care if he came early. There was nothing to be ashamed of, and she didn't really care to tease him as much as he had her. She wanted to taste him, every part of him.

She sped up. She pushed her nose all the way up to the little pit hair at the base. As she began to pull back before she choked, he thrust forward and held her head there as he ejaculated.

Slowly coming off him, she sucked him dry for everything he was worth, loving the taste and that he was able to get his release. Before she could swallow it all, he pulled her to her feet and kissed her.

"I love you," he said.

She was stunned by his declaration but felt it down in the deepest parts of her.

She said, "I love you too."

A smile stretched across his face like she had never seen before. She realized that in the past week, while she had been comforted and made to feel sure in his ability to keep the family together, he had been near hopeless. Now she saw hope and so much more in his face, taking up space in his eyes.

"So, I should move into your room then," AnnaLee said.

Sam pulled her closer to him. "Yeah, I suppose so."

"And we should probably talk to the girls about us, when we tell them everything else."

He nodded his head. "Probably."

"Good." She kissed him again.

SAM

The girls were more than delighted to know that their nanny and father were dating. More than dating. They were mates.

Emma and Jose wanted to call all of their uncles and aunts to tell them. Of course everyone said that they already knew. Even Ashton rolled his eyes and said it was obvious.

What the girls did not like was hearing that there was a small chance of them living with Jordan forever. Emma burst out in tears, wailing so loudly it sounded as if someone had died, and Jose's anger was so off the charts, neither AnnaLee nor Sam knew what to do. They knew to expect a reaction of extreme proportions, but this was more than either were prepared to do.

It took the entire day to calm them down and to remind them of the good things, such as AnnaLee and Sam being mated. Sam especially liked talking about that part. He was happy to be sleeping with AnnaLee and completely open about their relationship. He wanted to erase any doubts in anyone's mind about AnnaLee being his. He was hers.

After the girls had calmed down, Sam plowed ahead with the matter. He wanted to get it all done in one day rather than drag it out.

"We're telling you this, because how you interact with Jordan at the park will determine what happens," Sam said.

"You want us to scream at her," Jose said.

Sam almost said yes, but he knew that would be horrible. "No. Be nice like you would to someone you're just meeting."

"We are just meeting her," Emma said with a roll of her eyes.

"Then you should be fine."

AnnaLee said, "But if she scares you, you don't have to act unafraid. Be normal, and we'll win."

Both girls nodded their heads and said, "Okay."

It was a quick few days for all of them. They each wished it could have been slower, but before they knew it, they were all getting into the car with somber faces. No one had gotten much sleep the night before.

Both girls came running into Sam and AnnaLee's room. They snuggled up under the covers and started crying. Everyone was crying and trying to soothe each other.

The day was already dismal. The sky was gray with indecisive clouds, and a breeze made the sun absent day cold. Even though it was the end of summer, the sweaters they were in should have been unnecessary.

Thurshin was easy to find. Sam shook his hand, and Thurshin merely nodded his head at the girls. "Jordan should be here soon," Thurshin said.

Sam hoped Jordan wouldn't show at all, but that dream was short-lived when he spotted her jogging toward them.

"I came early to get a light jog in, before meeting the girls," she said. Her smile was radiant, but it didn't meet her eyes. Sam knew she was playing a game, but he didn't know what game it was. Aside from going to his house, she was following everything by the book.

She bent forward, her hands on her knees, to smile at the girls. "Hi Emma and Jose," she said.

Jose rolled her eyes. "I'm Jose. She's Emma."

Emma grabbed Jose's hand and stepped behind her.

"Do you want to go play on the playground?"

"We want to swing," Jose said.

Sam should have known she would take lead. She was practically shaking in her boots, but Emma was top priority to keep safe. If it came down to it, Jose would fight and Emma would scream, securing both of their safety.

He was not worried about them nearly as much as he should have been.

"Excellent! I can push," Jordan said.

Jose rolled her eyes again. "We know how to swing." She and Emma marched off toward the swing set.

Jordan stood and smiled wanly at Thurshin. "Girls, they're all like that."

"Not mine," AnnaLee said.

Jordan's smile instantly fell into disgust. "I'm sorry did you give birth to them?"

AnnaLee smiled, "I didn't need to."

Thurshin butted in and said, "Ladies enough. Jordan, I think the girls are in the playground without supervision."

Jordan straightened up. "Of course." She jogged after the girls.

Thurshin glared at AnnaLee, and Sam wanted to step in front of her and growl at him. She was protecting what was hers. She didn't need to be treated as if she was in the wrong.

"Let's sit down shall we," Thurshin motioned to a picnic table.

The silence that lingered around them was loud enough. No one liked the current situation. It was painful to watch, let alone be a part of.

Sam watched as Jordan stood in front of the swing set trying to make small talk with the girls who were blatantly ignoring her. Sam was proud of them for not being timid. Hopefully it worked in his favour.

"I can tell you right now she's off to a bad start," Thurshin said.

"So we win?" Sam was hopeful, but he knew what Thurshin's answer would be.

"Not by a long shot. Over the course of the next few minutes or even hours we could see the girls warming up to her. If that's the case."

He didn't need to finish his sentence. If the girls even showed signs of possibly liking Jordan, then Sam lost them. The familiar tight ache in his chest was back. He didn't want to breathe. He wasn't sure he remembered how to breathe.

AnnaLee's hand was on his back rubbing circles in easy breathing patterns. Left was inhale. Right was exhale.

"Could custody be split?" AnnaLee asked.

Thurshin shook his head. "Someone would have to move. Jordan and Sam live too far from each other, and I would never dream of putting that stress on the girls."

They all fell silent as they resumed watching Jordan interact with Emma and Jose.

Panic ran rampant in Sam's mind. He wondered if he would really be able to live with himself if Jordan won this. He would have to in the hopes of seeing them again and for the sake of his mate.

He was incredibly grateful for AnnaLee's presence. She held his hand tightly and pressed herself into his side. She was trying to provide a wall of assurance, and she did. Without her, he probably would have tried to fight Thurshin or even Jordan. Things would have gotten physical fast and then he really would have lost the girls. He wondered if he should set a date to go pick a fight with Dominick.

The man was a good friend to Sam, but he was as hot-headed as dragons could get. He was a bullish, bronze dragon and always aching for a fight. He wasn't a bad person, just lonely and stubborn.

It wouldn't be a bad idea to burn some of the emotion and energy with a good fight. If he wasn't mating his going at it as often as both he and his dragon craved, the fight would help settle him down.

Suddenly Emma came running up to the table. Sam's mind began jumping to conclusions. She was hurt, or Jose was hurt, and Jordan couldn't care for them.

Where was Jose? He quickly scanned the playground and found her hanging from the monkey bars with Jordan not far from her. He almost laughed at Jordan's waiting hands, expecting Jose to fall. The twins had been able to climb and hang by themselves since they were two.

"Can we get ice cream?" Emma asked AnnaLee.

"It's still a little early for ice cream," AnnaLee said.

Sam cocked his head and asked, "Why do you want ice cream?"

"Jordan said eating ice cream on a cold day is the perfect way to eat ice cream." Her head bobbed in every direction as she bounced on her toes.

Thurshin raised an eyebrow. "Do you agree with her?"

"No," Emma said.

"Emma, you'll hurt your teeth if we get ice cream," Sam said. "It happens every time."

"I won't bite the ice cream this time," she cried.

AnnaLee laughed. "Emma, you say that every time. No ice cream today, but maybe we can have chocolate waffles later."

She looked wary for a moment. The treat was definitely appealing to her. She cast her eyes around and looked at Jordan and Jose.

"You don't want it?" Thurshin asked.

"Do I have to share it with you and Jordan?" She looked incredibly concerned about the answer.

Sam said, "They won't be eating dinner with us, so no."

"Then I want it," she said. She nodded her head in confirmation to the dessert, and darted off toward her sister. She was already yelling about the yummy treat they would have later.

"Hmm." Thurshin made the sound, watching the girls closely.

"What?" Sam asked.

Thurshin waved his hand. "Nothing you need to worry about."

Sam was sure it was everything he needed to worry about. It was about his daughters, so he wanted to know. He wanted to know how what had just happened had affected things.

The play date couldn't end fast enough. The girls were exhausted, but they did not stop talking the whole time as they were buckled into their seats. AnnaLee waited in the car with the girls, but Sam had a hard time pulling his eyes away from them to talk to Thurshin and Jordan.

"Today was incredibly informative. I'm going back to my office, to think about things, but you two can expect a phone call from me in the next few days. We'll keep it quick and painless."

Jordan nodded her head, her eyes wide as if she just had the most interesting lecture of her life. Playing with twins probably was quite a learning experience, although she wouldn't have been so wonder-struck if she had been there from the beginning.

Not that Sam regretted her being gone. He was thankful for her absence; for leaving when she did. His daughters were committed to him and he to them, in ways he didn't think would have happened if Jordan had stayed around. He was also a much better person because she had left. Now he had AnnaLee. He never would have met his mate, if he was with Jordan.

Thurshin walked away leaving Jordan and Sam standing together. Sam stuck his hand out and said, "Thank you."

"What?" she looked taken aback and made no move to grab his hand.

"Thank you for leaving," he said, shoving his hands into his pockets. "I have the best family a man could ask for, all thanks to you being a horrible wife and mother."

"That's hardly fair," she said.

"I don't know why you're upset. I'm complimenting you."

"Hardly."

He shook his head and laughed.

"Do you know something I don't?" she asked, seething. Her eyes searched his face for any clue of what was going on.

"Yeah, I do. I know comfort and love; something I don't think you'll ever know because of your jealousy and paranoia."

"Excuse me?" Her hands were pathetic fists at her side.

"See you in Room C, when he calls us."

The car ride home was completely the opposite to the ride to the park. The girls did not stop talking. They never once mentioned a word about Jordan, but when Sam asked about her, the girls rolled their eyes and continued with their stories.

When they got home, AnnaLee sent them up to their rooms to

clean up for dinner, but neither girl came down. They were passed out on their beds, and AnnaLee and Sam were left to change them into pajamas.

Sam enjoyed dinner with AnnaLee. It was quiet but calming, something he needed. He needed a moment without worry about the current situation. It was nice to take a moment to shut his brain down and not think.

When he and AnnaLee retired to their room, he sat down on the edge of the bed and took deep, steadying breaths. AnnaLee crawled under the covers and watched him.

"You did good today," she said. Her voice was quiet and gentle.

"I was scared out of my mind." It was the truth, and he would only give her the truth.

"You didn't look like it." After a minute, she patted the blanket over her lap and said, "Come here Sam."

He turned over and crawled across the mattress towards her. He laid his head down on her lap and let her run her fingers through his hair. She didn't say anything, and he closed his eyes to keep focusing on controlling his breathing.

When morning came, Sam woke up to AnnaLee cradling his head to her breasts. Any other morning he would have turned the moment into a pre-breakfast feast, but the phone was ringing.

Slipping from her arms he pulled his phone off the nightstand and walked into the master bathroom. He looked into the mirror and was thankful whoever was calling couldn't see him. His face looked as if he had been hit with a brick.

He must have cried last night, because his eyes were puffy and there were clear tracks running down his cheeks. His mouth felt like cotton, so he quickly took a drink of water before finally answering the phone.

"Hello?"

"Sam, get AnnaLee and come down to the courthouse. We're doing things today." Thurshin's voice was urgent, sending Sam's heart into acrobatic stunts.

"Wait, are you sure?"

"Yes." Thurshin hung up without an explanation.

"Sam who is it?" AnnaLee called from the room.

He rushed in and pulled her from the bed. "We need to get dressed. Thurshin made his decision and we have to go."

"What about the girls?" AnnaLee was wide awake now, pulling on her pants from yesterday that she had discarded to the floor.

"Call Nora or Samia or whoever, but we need to go now."

ANNALEE

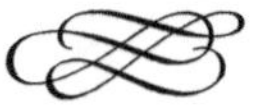

Nora came over as quickly as she could, and she shoved AnnaLee and Sam out of the house saying she was capable of watching the twins. She said not to come back until they won, even if Sam needed to breathe fire like a true dragon. AnnaLee didn't think breathing fire was possible, but in that moment she hoped it was.

The drive to the courthouse was tense. Neither Sam nor AnnaLee said anything in the hope that they wouldn't jinx the situation. Whatever had happened overnight was big.

AnnaLee didn't give herself time to think about what could have happened. There were too many unknowns that she would never be able to account for. She would just have to wait it out. They both would have to wait until they could speak to Thurshin.

The courthouse was already buzzing with activity when they arrived. It didn't concern them, but it created enough of a crowd that they had to shove their way through to get to the correct conference room. AnnaLee was ready to scream by the time they made it to the door.

Sam didn't knock or wait to be invited. He pushed through,

pulling AnnaLee right along with him. She kept one finger in a belt loop on the back of his pants so she didn't lose him.

Inside, Thurshin was already sitting down, his fingers steepled and pressed to his tightly sealed lips.

"Any sign of Jordan?" he asked. Sam and AnnaLee shook their heads. Thurshin nodded, expecting that response.

"Thurshin, what's going on?" Sam asked, sitting down next to him.

"She called me last night," he said. He pressed his lips together as if he was revealing secrets he wasn't supposed to spill.

AnnaLee didn't like the sound of Jordan calling him. She was up to no good and her absence in the room gave her an uneasy feeling. Something was wrong. It was too early for them to be meeting. No one should have been in the room. AnnaLee should have been home with the girls; she wasn't needed here.

"I need to go," she said. There was a familiar pull on her gut telling her to leave. It was the same feeling that had had her calling Sam the night before his re-evaluation. She was as connected to Emma and Jose as she was to Sam. She needed to follow this gut feeling.

"Wait, I'm sorry. I'm just shocked." Thurshin said.

"This isn't about your decision?" Sam asked.

"Yes and no," Thurshin said. "Jordan called me screaming threats. Clearly I'm not going to give in to that, but Sam, she screamed accusations about how you treat the girls, and if they're true no one will get them."

AnnaLee's heart plummeted. That was the worst, most unexpected news AnnaLee imagined she'd be hearing.

"Thurshin, you know how insane that is," Sam said.

"Of course I do," he scoffed. "I've known you for a long time, and I know none of what she said to be true, but I'm trying to do my job and get the full scope of things here."

"Where's Jordan then?" AnnaLee asked. "She should be here to point her finger herself. She doesn't need you for that."

Thurshin shook his head, pressing his lips together again.

"Where's Jordan?" Sam pushed.

"I called her right after I hung up with you, but she didn't pick up her phone. I called her several times and left several voicemails saying if she didn't make it here, she would lose all chances."

AnnaLee sucked in a breath. That was the good news she was hoping for.

"If she cannot defend her case," Thurshin continued, "then she doesn't have one."

The gut feeling intensified, similar to period cramps, and AnnaLee almost bent over. She needed to get home.

"I'm not needed here though," AnnaLee said.

Sam looked at her with his eyes drawn together. Even Thurshin was confused.

"No," Thurshin said. "You're not, but I thought you would want to be with him."

"I do, but the girls," she trailed off, unsure of how to explain what she was feeling.

Thurshin nodded his head as if he understood, although AnnaLee highly doubted it. In fact, she was amazed Sam wasn't feeling the same way she was. Instead, he looked confused, but was willing to respect her desire to leave.

"Is everything okay?" Sam asked, grabbing her hand as she rose from her chair.

Before she could answer her phone rang. The caller ID was Nora, and if AnnaLee's heart could have sunk any lower it would have. She knew that whatever Nora had to say would not be good.

"Nora, be quick about it."

She took deep breaths, and squeezed Sam's hand.

It was as if the world had suddenly stopped. Nothing was spinning, beating, or ticking anymore. It was like being in the doctor's office, feeling as if her head was underwater and everything he said was muffled.

Nora's voice was muffled, because it couldn't be true. The panic and despair couldn't be true. AnnaLee's phone slipped from her hand. Sam wasn't fast enough getting out of his chair, and AnnaLee's knees hit the floor with a resounding thud.

Sam was in front of her in seconds, and Thurshin rushed to her side. They were both talking to her, but they might as well have been on a different planet. For a moment, AnnaLee had considered it a miracle. Despite the fibroids, she managed to get daughters. Strong, beautiful daughters, and she had fallen in love with their father, who loved her back.

It was the perfect set up for a fairy tale. She hoped this one still had a chance at a happy ending, but her hope was quickly slipping between her fingers, while giving devastating rope burn on her heart and mind.

"Nora, speak to me now," Sam's voice drew AnnaLee's attention back to the moment.

While Nora explained the situation to Sam, AnnaLee looked at Thurshin and said, "I've simultaneously found and lost Jordan."

Thurshin's face turned white.

AnnaLee said, "Nora only took a moment to drink some water, but it was long enough for Jordan to dart across the yard and grab them."

Sam hung up the phone and placed it on the table. She could see in his face that he was trying hard not to break apart as she had. He was holding himself together for her, for Emma and Jose.

"Jordan didn't go to the backyard. She walked straight through the front door."

"She kidnapped them?" Thurshin asked.

Sam nodded his head.

"If it's any consolation," Thurshin said, "you win. They are your girls, and I suggest we start looking for them."

Sam helped AnnaLee to her feet. He looked at her, while wiping the tears from her cheeks. He cupped her face and said, "Nora's already called Cain, and every able-bodied person will be on this case."

She knew what he meant. Every dragon and shifter they could enlist would be out sniffing for their kids.

She nodded her head, gulping down her rising tears. "We should fly over the city," she said.

If it wasn't for the reason why they were flying, she might have liked riding him.

They met up with the rest of the dragons and they all shifted, scattering into the air to cover a wider range of the city, looking for Jordan. The other women took their cars, following their dragons from the ground. AnnaLee was the only one who decided to ride in the air with her mate.

The air was so much sweeter up in the sky. It wrapped around AnnaLee like a cool blanket greeting an old friend. AnnaLee tilted her head back and took in a deep breath relishing the feeling of the moment.

She let the fresh air fill her lungs and relax her nerves. It sharpened her focus and her resolve to find the girls.

It was dangerous flying during the day. Anyone could spot a giant dragon flying in the sky and quickly get a news report on it. They had to be careful and incredibly stealthy, following whichever way the clouds drifted.

Hours and minutes ticked by, building one on top of the other and increasing AnnaLee's anxiety. By the time dinner time came around, every dragon was exhausted, and AnnaLee could barely stand.

Nora and Samia wrapped their arms around AnnaLee, holding her up. They were all supporting each other. The twins had a much larger family than just AnnaLee and Sam and everyone was worried about them.

"We need to eat and then we can go back out," Harper said. Marshall wrapped an arm around his mate's waist and kissed her forehead.

Everyone nodded in agreement.

AnnaLee wanted to object, but she could barely keep her legs under her let alone say anything against good food and good rest.

They all sat in Cain and Nora's living room discussing what would be best to do next.

Again, it was like being underwater. Everything was muffled and unclear. All AnnaLee could think about was the girls being frightened. From the moment that Jordan had stepped into their house, the girls knew to be scared. AnnaLee should have trusted their original reaction. She should have fought more against them having time with Jordan.

Her head felt dizzy and her stomach moved in a way that had AnnaLee quickly covering her mouth. She shot off the couch she was on and darted for the bathroom. She slammed the door behind her and bent over the toilet.

Sam banged on the door. "AnnaLee, what's wrong?"

She should have known he would be close on her heels, but she still didn't open the door. She heaved the contents of her stomach into the toilet bowl and continued to dry heave until the smell was too much for her to slump there. She flushed the toilet and leaned back against the closed door.

Sam continued to knock. His voice had grown stressed as he panicked over her absence, and the distance that the door created. She felt the same way, and itched to let him in, but she needed a minute to breathe, and to be away from all that they were saying.

One breath.

Two breaths.

Her phone rang.

The caller ID was unknown, but something told her to answer it. Whatever the universe was telling her now, she would not ignore it.

"Hello?" Her voice was surprisingly strong considering how she felt.

"AnnaLee," the voice said her name with disgust. Jordan said her name with disgust.

"Jordan," AnnaLee said with relief. If Jordan was calling, then there was hope. "Should I get Sam?"

"No, I've talked to him enough. I want to talk to you, his mate." She spat the word mate as if it was some horrible disease.

Outside the door, Sam had gone quiet, probably listening in to the phone call as best he could. AnnaLee remembered pestering him one night for all the details of special skills that came with being a dragon. She remembered him saying superior hearing was one of the better things that dragons had.

"What do you want with me?"

"Just to talk. Get in your car and drive to the location I'm going to send you." Jordan hung up and sent an address.

AnnaLee was out of the bathroom, and stumbling past Sam's arms to get to her car. Sam followed her without saying a word.

AnnaLee reached her car. Sam was going to follow her into the car when she stopped him. "No, fly," she said.

He nodded his head, and shifted quickly, leaping into the air.

Looking over her shoulder, she saw everyone waiting in the doorway, watching. She gave them a wan smile of hope, before driving away.

She plugged the address into her GPS and sped through the neighborhood and onto the highway. It led to an old, shut-down road stop. The thought of the girls being somewhere so dark and creepy sent chills along AnnaLee's spine.

Her phone rang again.

"Jordan, quit the games."

"It's not a game AnnaLee, it's life."

"I don't accept that." AnnaLee shook her head. This was all Jordan's game and they were playing by her rules.

"Would you believe me if I said I really did want my daughters?" Jordan's voice cracked.

"No," AnnaLee said. It was the truth. Jordan wouldn't have acted so monstrously if she were being honest.

"Well it's true. I wanted to see them and Sam." The laugh that crackled through the phone was dry.

"He and I were always fighting for obvious reasons. When I was pregnant, I knew before they were born that I would have to hunt them someday. I knew when they were in my womb that they were shifters.

I didn't need to wait twelve damned years to find out, but I was going to wait that long, and give them a chance at life, before I added their names to my list. Then Sam was stupid enough to ask for a re-evaluation. I told myself that I was going to look at them and leave, but you were there.

The fire that lanced through my body when I saw you clutching those girls was more than I had ever felt before. I wanted to help purify you of being his mate, but I was also horrified by my repulsion toward my own daughters. The park was supposed to help."

AnnaLee cut in and said, "Let me guess, it didn't."

Jordan laughed again. "No, it didn't. I knew Thurshin was going to let them stay with Sam, and if I was going to help purify the world at all, this would be my one chance."

"What have you done, Jordan?"

All AnnaLee could see were images of the girls being cut up and strewn across a parking lot or stuffed into a trunk while carbon monoxide filled it and poisoned their lungs. The most gruesome deaths imaginable were what AnnaLee imagined being done to the twins.

"They're there. Unharmed."

"What?" AnnaLee couldn't believe what she was hearing.

"As a hunter, I'm a magical anomaly. I might very well burst into flames for not doing my job, but whether you believe me or not, I did love Sam and I had dreamed of loving Emma and Jose."

Jordan fell silent waiting for AnnaLee's response. She needed to respond. Despite what Jordan said, she wanted AnnaLee's approval, and belief in her.

"Okay," AnnaLee said. She couldn't give more than that.

"Okay," Jordan said.

"I still hate you, and given the chance I'd bring you to the same demise as I give all shifters."

"Good to know."

"AnnaLee?"

"Yeah, Jordan?"

"Don't let them look for me when they're older. You birthed them, the end."

That was all AnnaLee would ever get from Jordan. It was as good as her okay.

"Okay."

Jordan hung up.

AnnaLee pulled off the highway, the unused road crackling

beneath her tires. Her headlights shone around the abandoned area, and she looked for the two tiny forms frantically that would indicate her daughters.

She slammed on the brakes and threw the gear shift into park. As she swung out of the car, Sam landed next to her, and they started yelling for the girls.

"Emma!" AnnaLee yelled.

"Jose!" Sam followed.

They ran circles around the old building, pulling on the locked doors, looking for busted windows. There was no way the girls were inside, so where were they?

"Mommy!" A cry came from close to the highway.

"Daddy!" Jose's voice followed.

Sam and AnnaLee skidded to a halt and bolted toward the sounds. They kept calling for each other until Sam and AnnaLee scooped the girls into their arms and held them close. They petted the girls' hair and whispered into their ears that they were safe, peppering their foreheads, cheeks, and hands with reassuring kisses. They wiped away their tears and promised they would never be lost or so afraid again.

Taking the girls back to the car, Sam sat in the driver's seat and AnnaLee remained in the back, holding both girls to her.

*J*ordan was gone. Cain sent out feelers in every direction, calling in favors from more shifter clans than Sam knew of. Whatever had happened, no one would see her again for a very long time, if ever.

It was difficult at first to accept, but AnnaLee held his face, kissed him, and said, "We are here and together and that will not change. Now, be present with your family."

He tried. He still woke up during the night, just to check Emma and Jose's rooms. They were always soundly asleep, and AnnaLee was always there too. Sometimes AnnaLee would sleep with Emma or Jose and sometimes she would stay curled up soundly next to him.

Their family was complete.

Sam walked into his room. AnnaLee's lamp was casting a golden glow around the room. The girls had just lain down, and they were getting ready for bed themselves.

"Thurshin said he would mail us the signed papers, so we don't have to go up to the courthouse," AnnaLee said from her place tucked beneath the blankets.

"Hmm," Sam mused.

"Do you know what that means?"

"What?" He looked up from where he was glancing at his phone screen and froze.

AnnaLee flipped the blankets off of her revealing her naked body to him. "You made me a promise Sam."

He didn't need more of an invitation than that. He took off his clothes, and eagerly crawled on top of her. He settled between her legs, and looked lovingly into her eyes.

"You are beautiful," he said.

He brushed a strand of hair from her forehead and leaned his head down to kiss her. He tilted her chin to gain better access. Practiced dance partners now, their tongues swirled together, loving every part of each other.

He kissed the tip of her nose, her lips, her chin, and down her throat to the base of her neck, before gladly pursuing each nipple. He pulled their pebbled peaks into his mouth and lathered his tongue over them, gently nipping with his teeth.

He had brought her to completion so many times at this point that he could draw her blind, but still her body seemed new, and reacted differently each time. There was always a better way he could please her, a new way he could touch her. He loved learning what made her squirm and loved watching her writhe beneath him.

He kissed the valley between her breasts, her stomach, her navel, and the light patch of hair at the apex between her thighs. He could smell her desire and knew she was ready, but he still worked slowly back up to her lips, where he claimed her again.

"Sam," she gasped. "Please don't make me wait a minute longer."

He obliged willingly. He settled between her legs, positioned himself at her entry point, and in a quick thrust entered her to the hilt. He slowly pulled out and thrust himself back in, enjoying the sounds of their bodies colliding like worlds that were meant to merge and become one.

He reached between them and began to shower her button with pulses and caresses. "Come with me now, baby."

He worked her to a high point, from where they fell together.

Sam collapsed beside her, and drew her close, keeping himself inside of her.

"I love you," he said.

She patted his shoulder in response, still looking for a coherent thought in her shattered mind.

"Me too," she finally managed.

The sound of her breathy voice filled him with satisfaction. He loved knowing he had made her sound like that.

She gasped and hit his shoulder. "Sam, I can't go again, so soon."

Indeed, he was already growing inside her. He laughed and rolled over, nuzzling his nose into her neck, and getting himself high on her scent.

"I think I'll be the judge of what you're capable of."

She laughed, and arched her back as he kissed her fluttering pulse.

EPILOGUE

There wasn't enough Scotch in the world to hold his battering thoughts at bay or the appeal of the bartender's swaying hips. God, he had fingered those hips and the hem of her shorts enough times to know they were soft as velvet. Likewise, he had been thrown out of the bar and slapped enough times to know the owner of those hips was not interested.

She was the only damned girl who was not interested in him.

Dominick could pick any girl in the bar, and he often did, but they were all weak and gentle. He wanted the bartender, who could sling a drink down the bar with such precision his dragon was impressed. His eyes followed her every movement, but he wasn't sure he could copy it that perfectly, even if he practiced.

"What are you doing here?" she accused, wiping the already pristine counter in front of him.

He cocked his head to the side and smirked. "Friend's got a new mate," he said.

"Oh, how sad for you." She rolled her eyes and walked away from him.

Good. Let her walk away. He could watch one of his other favorite assets about her. It barely fit in her shorts and begged for him to bury himself there.

The thought was not unusual, but for some reason it jarred him. He didn't like it. He was mad at himself for thinking so lewdly about her.

He needed a fight.

"Lilly, slide me another," he raised his glass to show her what he wanted, although she always knew what he was drinking. He had tried to change it up one night, and before he could even tell her, she guessed his order to a T.

"Careful, Dom. You'll get wrecked if you have more," she said, handing it to him rather than sliding it.

"Good," he said. "That's the plan."

He knocked back the drink, not even noticing the burn anymore. Nothing kept him warm and only pain kept him numb at this point.

Lilly shook her head. "At least die outside, okay. No one wants to haul your body out of here."

He winked. "Except you."

"Ugh, I think I just puked in my mouth."

She said that now, but he was determined. He'd get her. Until then, a fight would have to do.

He slammed cash onto the counter and left heading toward wolf territory, where a good fight was always to found.

* * *

The End

Did you like this book? Then you'll LOVE Wolf Dad's Mate, the first book in The Wolf Dad's Love Chronicles.

Click here and get Wolf Dad's Mate!

. . .

***THE BOND** between a wolf and his woman is stronger than anything.*

After their exes are exposed for the liars they are, Sofia and Max are able to finally kindle their love in public. But one thing divides them: Max is a powerful wolf shifter and Sofia is just a human. In this story of love and betrayal, no one is safe unless they become powerful enough to shift.

Sofia and Max will stop at nothing to protect their love, including taking risks that will put them both in danger. After they are both betrayed by their exes, it seems no matter where the couple travel, they'll always be at risk.

Sofia and Max will never stop fighting for their love, and they aren't alone—they have a strong group of shifters to back them up and support their romance.

Wolf Dad's Love Chronicles Book 1: The Wolf Dad's Mate is bound to make you sweat.

START READING Wolf Dad's Mate **NOW!**

WOLF DAD'S MATE SNEAK PEEK

Sofia walked the long halls of the planetarium, her pink heels making clicking noises against the marble floor. She had lost track of her boyfriend, Jameson, ages ago. He was probably flirting with one of the obnoxious wait staff, who continually asked him, in their bubbly voices, if he would like another canapé; they were made *especially* for him by the chef.

"What?" He had said to Sofia when she'd given him a look. "It's just food. It's not going to hurt anyone."

The waitress had giggled as well, and Sofia had rolled her eyes. She knew Jameson had cheated on her, but she hadn't confronted him about it yet. Why upheave her entire life all because of some vapid women? She didn't want to give up her apartment looking over Boston's city lights, or the hot tub in the living room.

It wasn't that Sofia was vapid as well, either. She was just lonely, and having Jameson around was better than having no one. Besides, she got to visit the new planetarium he had recently taken part in funding, before it got too crowded.

The hallway was covered in enormous orbs of light with tiny stars attached to them. Ahead was an enormous painting of what she assumed were the Greek gods come to life, the lines of constellations vaguely outlining their bodies. They were reaching for each other in an enormous galaxy, filled with stars and suns; the oil paint thick in some places, thin in others.

If the painting wasn't hanging so far above her head she would have loved to have lifted a hand up to touch it.

"Beautiful, huh?" came a voice from behind her that sounded distinctly *unlike* Jameson.

Sofia whipped around to look at the stranger who had the nerve to speak to her and found herself face to face with a tall and handsome man.

He was muscular and his hair had grown out enough that he could run his hands through it. His beard was scruffy. but not too long and his eyes were a piercing blue.

"I'm sorry, what did you say?" Sofia laughed.

She felt herself blushing, so distracted was she with this man's appearance. She'd never seen anyone like him – at least not in Cambridge, where everyone was either a skinny biker or a coffee barista. Except Jameson – she supposed he was strong, but what did that matter.

The man chuckled softly and Sofia felt the icy castle around her heart melting ever so slightly.

"I asked if you thought the painting was beautiful"

"I do," Sofia said. "I was just admiring the stars – you know, it's the strangest thing, I wanted to reach out and touch it so badly, but I'm far too short to—"

"Ah, say no more," the mysterious man said.

Without another word he closed the space between himself and Sofia, and then he lifted her up so that she could touch the painting. She didn't protest, thinking about how warm his arms were around her legs.

She let her right hand reach out to the painting. The oil paint was just as she remembered it, smooth in some spots, sticking up in plasticky ridges like waves in a frozen ocean. She could only touch the goddess's foot, but she did so just in case it brought her any good luck.

The man slowly let Sofia out of his arms, until they were face to face for a split second. Sofia found she couldn't look away from his eyes. They were like waking up on a winter's day to find that it had snowed the night before and everything was covered in chilly crystals.

Her mom was still alive and she was baking sugar cookies in the other room, placing electric blue sprinkles on their surfaces.

"Darling!" boomed a voice from the other end of the hall.

"Guess I should be going," the mysterious man said.

"Wait, I don't even know what your name is," Sofia said.

He chuckled again. "Don't worry; we'll see each other again soon."

He began to walk in the opposite direction, nodding at Jameson as they crossed paths.

"Do we know him?" Jameson asked as he approached Sofia.

She couldn't read the look on his face.

"No, we do not know him. He was just helping me—I tripped, and I thought I hurt my ankle."

"Aw," Jameson said.

It sounded, to Sofia, as if he was mocking her ever so slightly.

"You ready to go, babe?" Sofia asked.

"Actually, I was just coming to ask if you wanted me to call you a car. Some of us are going out to the bar to celebrate the success of the planetarium. You didn't want to go, did you?"

Sofia rolled her large hazel eyes. Of course, Jameson was going somewhere without her. She was just arm candy to him, and more like baggage these days.

"No," she said wearily. "Just call me a car. I'll meet you back at the apartment."

"Excellent," he said, swooping in to kiss her on the cheek. "Don't wait up."

He turned on his heel, his feet clad in expensive black alligator leather, and she followed him out of the room like a lost puppy.

When they got to the front entrance she scanned every stranger's face, but couldn't find the blue-eyed man anywhere. It was as if he had disappeared like a cloud of mist. Surely, he lived around here—maybe if she visited again tomorrow, he might show up.

Who was she kidding? He wasn't interested in her. Of course, Sofia was gorgeous, but as Jameson put it, she had more of a subtle good look to her. She was curvy and tall, with dark-blond hair and lightly tanned skin, passed down from her Italian heritage.

That night, she was wearing pink pumps and a black dress covered in gemstones that reminded her of the stars in the sky. She was more of a romantic than anything, and chose to live each part of her life as if she were the heroine in an incredibly mysterious story.

But, this story seemed like it was ending with her getting into a stained, blue taxicab and heading home alone.

"I'll see you later," Jameson said as she slid into the backseat.

He dismissively tapped the roof of the car twice and it drove off. He didn't even kiss her goodbye.

In the back of the taxi, Sofia slid into the comfort of the leather and imagined she was leaning against the handsome stranger. He would have kissed her goodbye. Hell, he probably would have gotten into the cab with her. She didn't deserve to be left alone by Jameson all the time.

Outside, the sky was cloudy; there weren't even any stars to look at. Sofia leaned on her side and watched as the buildings rushed past. They were a mixture of brightly-lit and completely dark. Surprisingly, some businesses were still open, even though Boston tended to close down earlier than any other city she'd lived in before.

When she got to her apartment, she fumbled with her keys. She hadn't had anything to drink, but she was exhausted and she wanted to take her heels off. Jameson wasn't around, so she slid her heels off right there, and let her feet rest on the cool sidewalk.

To her left, she thought she saw a pair of eyes. Upon closer inspection, she saw an enormous, white wolf lurking in the trees, in the park near her apartment. She stopped dead in her tracks. She was inches away from the doorway; she could make a run for it. But, the wolf was big, it might catch her.

To her surprise it blinked once and then disappeared into the brush.

"That was strange," Sofia said, before letting herself into her apartment.

CLICK HERE and get Wolf Dad's Mate!